MW00834434

LUNAR NIGHT

PAMELA R. SMITH

KAKAROT BELMONT

This novel is a work of fiction. Names, characters, places, and incidents are either the product of the author's imagination or are used fictitiously and any resemblance to actual persons, living or dead is entirely coincidental.

Copyright © 2019 Pamela R. Smith
Cover Art by Warren Design
Library of Congress Cataloging-in-Publication Data is available.

All rights reserved. No part of this book may be reproduced, stored in a retrieval system, or transmitted in any form or by any means, electronic, mechanical, photocopying, recording, or otherwise without written permission of the author.

ISBN-13: 978-0-9884540-3-3 (paperback)
ISBN-13: 978-0-9884540-4-0 (eBook)

First Edition, April 2019

Published by Kakarot Belmont
Printed in the United States of America

When it is dark enough, you can see the stars.

- RALPH WALDO EMERSON

Chapter One

The darkness was complete, obsidian. He knew instinctively nothing could penetrate this kind of darkness. Crouching at the back of the cave, he waited, peering into the darkness. Unable to see, his awareness kicked up a notch and he perceived that something was out there. He knew they were out there because they only came out at night. Looking down at his empty hands, he wondered why he had no weapons. And no light. They hated light. Frantically he searched his pockets for his flashlight. Nothing. Confused and disoriented, he could not fathom why he was there.

Out of the deadly silence, he heard them. Night stalkers, climbing up the side of the hill directly toward him. Toward this cave. He knew the night stalkers lived in caves. Was he hiding in their lair? Heart madly racing, his terror increased. He squinted into the darkness as footsteps drew near. At the cave entrance, a pair of yellow eyes appeared, glaring at him. Then another, and another, until it seemed like hundreds of yellow eyes filled the entrance to the cave. He drew back in horror as their screams pierced the air, and they clambered noisily over each other to reach him. Their stench filled his nostrils as they enveloped him.

Tanner woke with a start, tangled in his bedding. With his heart racing and sweat beading on his forehead, he threw his blanket aside and peered around. The first shafts of sunlight brightened the sky in swirling fingers of brilliant orange and yellow. His campfire smoldered with the last embers of a dying fire.

Sitting up, Tanner touched the rifle by his side, reassured by its presence. As he calmed down, his heart rate slowly returned to normal. It was just a dream. The early morning light assured him he was safe from the dread of nightfall and the seemingly endless night when the stalkers roamed.

He broke camp quickly, and eyeing the distant steps that slashed up the mountainside, decided he would take a detour before returning home. Wanting the best view, he knew the steps would take him to the top of the mountain and he could easily survey his surroundings. He needed more information.

Two hours later, he stood gazing up the steep incline. With hundreds of unevenly spaced railroad ties, it was nothing less than a staircase up the mountain. Tanner could not recollect when he had last been on the steps.

Two thousand feet up and a mile long, it had once been a popular fitness destination for those craving an intense workout. His father had joked about it being a rite of passage for athletes training for the Olympics. Now it was

2

simply a necessity to reach the top and obtain the best view of the surrounding area.

When he was a young boy, Tanner's father brought him up here to share in a challenging hike. People crowded the steps and he remembered the voices of camaraderie as they cheered one another on.

No voices now, only a slight cooling breeze blowing gently through the trees. The steps were deserted and in disrepair, with many of the ties broken or gone, and human camaraderie was in short supply and now valuable beyond measure.

Tanner slung his rifle over his shoulder and stopped at the sign near the bottom of the steps. He could barely read the weathered wording: The Incline will be temporarily closed for repairs August 31st thru Oct 1st 2021. Twenty years ago and the repairs were never completed, the staircase all but forgotten. At the time, survival had been more important.

It still was, he reminded himself, as he felt again the urgency to get to the top. As he passed the sign, another one lay broken and dirty on the ground. He bent down and brushed off the dirt to read the words: Elevation-6500 feet. How high will be enough, he wondered, as he rose and began the ascent, slowly climbing the crumbling staircase.

Stopping about two thirds of the way to the top of the incline, Tanner took a long draught of water from his canteen. He was now at the bailout point where Barr Trail, the winding path west of the staircase, came close enough to get on and head back down. A tired hiker, unwilling or unable to continue, could take the trail back from here. He glanced at the still intact walkway and railing that lead from the incline to the trail. Memories surfaced.

As a boy, he had bailed out at this point. His dad's words echoed in his mind, "Son, you can do it. You got this far."

He had replied with a shake of his head.

Although disappointed, his father had patted his back enthusiastically and smiled, "I'll meet you at the bottom then." Tanner only nodded.

When his father trudged on up the stairs and out of sight, he had pulled out his cell phone and continued a game that the hike had interrupted. If only he'd known how little time was left with his father. Tanner pushed the thought aside. Regret would not help him now.

Pulling binoculars out of his backpack, he scanned the area to the east, across the shattered city, and toward the plains beyond. He turned slightly, scanning to the south, still no sign of water.

His rover, Tweeny, had insisted the water was approaching. With dread knotting his stomach, Tanner contemplated the ramifications of that. He needed more time, more time to prepare.

The afternoon air was turning warmer. Wiping his sweaty forehead, Tanner splashed some water on his face and continued his upward climb. A half hour later, breathing hard from the exertion, he was at the top. Immediately, he pulled the binoculars out and scanned to the south and east once again.

No bluish tinge on the horizon, only brown prairie. No water in sight. Not yet, anyway. He breathed a sigh of relief.

Tweeny had traveled into the panhandle of Oklahoma six months ago when he came across rovers from Texas scouting the area. Desperate for dry land, they told him the destroyed city of Houston was inundated, and the water was slowly moving north and was now lapping the southern outskirts of Dallas. Migrating bands of survivors were being pushed northward. According to the rovers, California was submerged and the water was rising up the mountains. Tanner was hopeful if the water did reach this far, their elevation would be high enough to protect them.

After scouring the horizon, Tanner reluctantly brought his focus to the destruction below. The city of Colorado Springs, once nestled comfortably against the backdrop of the Rocky Mountains, lay below him destroyed and desolate, buildings and streets in ruin. It had not taken a direct hit in the beginning; it was only later that the destruction had been complete. No sign of movement, the ruined city abandoned years ago, the mountain range now a silent sentinel keeping watch over a dead city.

Although tenuous, life was springing back. There were a couple of small settlements, one by the river and one farther north close to the old academy. A few bands of people eked out a meager existence living and foraging along the river from east of Pueblo to south of Denver. They managed to get by. How much longer?

The rivers were drying up because it no longer snowed in the winter and there was no run off. The beginning of summer had been wet which helped, but so far late summer and fall had been dry since the end of July.

As he gazed at the remains of the city, memories swept through him like a gale. Ten years after the destruction, a small band of people lived and began to flourish along the river in the southern part of the city. One day that had all changed. Unknowingly, they brought a scourge into their midst when they welcomed a stranger into their small settlement.

He recalled how he and his grandfather had traveled there to trade some goods and instead found everyone in the new settlement dead with the telltale pox on their faces and bodies. Not one had survived. Fortunately, his grandfather had recognized the speckled monster before either of them touched a body.

Being a doctor, his grandfather had been horrified that smallpox, one of the deadliest pathogens known to man, had reappeared in the world once again. He explained to Tanner that smallpox had been successfully eradicated throughout the world. All known stocks destroyed or transferred to one of two secured laboratories in either Atlanta in the United States or Koltsovo, Russia. These two labs had been the only ones authorized to hold stocks of live smallpox virus. Was the virus once again let loose in the world, with no way to contain it?

Did someone purposely do this or was one of the labs housing the virus destroyed and the vials compromised? Could infected people have carried it across the continent? If so, was it possible that virulent contagion may have been released into the environment? Every question brought mounting fear with the terror of their discovery.

Tanner's grandfather insisted on burning the bodies to contain the virus. To avoid contact with the corpses, they had used old HAZMAT suits purchased long ago during an Ebola scare. Piling the diseased, rotting bodies of men, women, and children on top of one another, they set them afire. It had been a bonfire of death. Then, they had burned the settlement. It was a night he would never forget. In all the years since, they had not seen a reoccurrence of a smallpox outbreak.

A sudden snap of a twig behind him brought his mind cascading back to the present. Heart jumping, he quickly whirled around, at the same time bringing the rifle up, finger on the trigger. A deer bounded out of the trees and up the trail. Tanner lowered his rifle, pounding heart still hammering in his chest.

Taking a deep breath and slowly releasing a long exhalation, Tanner steadied himself. He watched the deer disappear back into the woods as his racing heart slowly returned to normal. He couldn't let his guard down like that. It could be deadly.

Needing to go no farther up, he decided to descend on the winding trail rather than back down the unsafe, broken steps. He took a short rest and ate some dried meat. The trail was just a few yards from the top of the steps and continued up the mountain all the way to Pikes Peak, the highest mountain in the area, usually covered with snow by now.

After taking one last cursory glance around, he strode toward the trail, senses heightened, rifle ready. His long, swinging stride took him back down the mountain quickly. There were times when rocks and tree limbs blocked the trail and he had to veer off or jump over obstacles, but the trail was still fairly well preserved unlike much of everything else.

Approaching the end of the trail, senses alert for anything out of the ordinary, he felt the hair on his neck rise. Stopping dead in his tracks, he listened intently, but there was nothing. Still feeling a little on edge after the sudden appearance of the deer, he cautiously stepped around a large rock in the middle of the trail and abruptly stopped.

Directly in front of him, in the middle of the trail, lay a body. Not just the normal dead body he was used to seeing, but this one appeared to be alive and breathing, although sleeping or unconscious. Tanner approached with caution, looking around, aware of everything but hearing only the quiet chirping of small birds in the trees. He knew instinctively there was no one else in the area.

Kneeling down, he checked for a pulse and found a strong one. Relieved, he gently turned the body over and was surprised to find the petite shape of a woman. With the brown jacket, slacks, and dark ski cap pulled over her head, she had looked like a small man.

He felt for broken bones and noticed a deep cut on her forearm where her jacket sleeve had ripped open and dried blood surrounded the wound. Pulling off her cap to gently probe her skull, he felt a large bump on the back of her head. There was also dried blood on this wound and in her cap, so she could possibly be suffering from a concussion. Although knocked unconscious, he saw no signs of a scuffle. One thing was certain; she did not appear to be waking up.

Feeling confident she had no broken bones, Tanner turned his attention to her face. He had not seen anyone like her in a long time. Her long auburn hair was pulled back tight in a knot at the back of her head and her face drew his attention with its unblemished, porcelain complexion, making her seem childlike, although she looked to be in her mid twenties. It was a face that was devoid of the hardship and stress of the last twenty years which he was sure was written all over his face.

With a multitude of questions running through his head, he gently picked her up. She was so light. Tanner knew he could get them back to the settlement and home before nightfall, as he was less than two hours from home. He certainly didn't want to be out here when the sun went down because it was definitely not safe in the darkness of night and it was always profoundly dark at night.

The illuminating lights of the cities had been extinguished. If only it had just been the lights, he thought, staggering slightly with an overwhelmingly sense of loss.

Shoving his thoughts aside, he glanced at the woman in his arms. Where could she have come from? Women didn't just fall from the sky. He glanced up as if needing reassurance of that.

Shaking off his foolishness, he carefully started off, trying not to jar her too much while maintaining a fast pace. His thoughts once again strayed to the unlikelihood of finding someone unconscious and alone on the mountainside, especially a woman.

Chapter Two

It was late afternoon by the time Tanner arrived home. Approaching the deep woods surrounding the settlement and home, he softly chirped twice and received an answering peep. A guard was out, but Tanner didn't see him and that was good; the guard was doing his job. As he approached the cabin, Tweeny the rover jumped up from his position by the empty campfire pit and gaped at Tanner.

"You got a live one?"

Ignoring Tweeny, Tanner walked past him to the entrance of the cabin. He hastily threw the door open and entered. His grandfather, sitting at the table drinking some strange-smelling brew, glanced up.

Looking like the wizard from an old Merlin picture he once had on his bedroom wall, Tanner always expected him to pick up a wand and start swirling it in the air. Though he was Doctor Marvin Lane, Tanner had always called him Grandpa Merlin; with his wavy long silver hair and beard, the name had stuck and now he was known as Merlin the Magician because a doctor was as close to a magician as one could get these days.

Tanner made for the cot in the corner, next to a doorway into the bedroom of the cabin. He gently laid the unconscious female down. Her face was pale and drawn and she neither opened her eyes nor moved.

"If I may inquire, what have we here?" Merlin asked, getting up and approaching the cot. Tanner knew she was in safe hands because his grandfather was the best damn doctor around, probably the only damn doctor around.

"I found her on the trail coming back from the incline," he answered. "There doesn't appear to be any broken bones."

Looking down at the unconscious woman, Merlin frowned. He gently prodded her and examined the wound on her head.

"It looks like she has a good sized bump on her head." Merlin gently lowered her head and lifted her arm to examine the deep cut. "This will need stitches." He felt along her side and noticed a slight protrusion in one of her pants pockets. "Huh, what's this?"

Tanner's head jerked up. Merlin pulled a small object from her pocket, frowning as he scrutinized it. Tanner gazed curiously at the object in his grandfather's hand.

"What is it?"

"Well," Merlin responded, as he turned the small item in his hand. "Looks like we now know her name."

He walked over to Tanner and handed him what looked like a card. Puzzled, Tanner studied it, turning it over in his hand. One word was on the front, Elizabeth. The back had some kind of code on it.

Tanner's eyes narrowed, "It looks like an identification card. In today's world, who would need that? To our knowledge, only small bands of people remain. Certainly, no companies with employees."

Merlin walked over to the cupboard and grabbed some medical supplies to clean the wounds. As he worked, he glanced over at Tanner. "Only one place around here had security like that, Cheyenne Mountain."

"Cheyenne Mountain?" Tanner looked at his grandfather in disbelief. "That was destroyed, almost at the beginning of the aftermath. Remember the two workers who barely escaped when it collapsed."

"Maybe it didn't completely collapse," Merlin responded quietly.

Tanner saw something flicker in the depths of Merlin's eyes; then, it was gone. Regardless of what his grandfather hoped, Tanner did not believe anyone could have survived the destruction of the military complex within Cheyenne Mountain.

Merlin began stitching up the wound on his patient's forearm. When he was done, he poured antiseptic over it and put a clean bandage on.

"Don't want it to get infected," he murmured. "Not much left in the way of antibiotics until Frank comes up with

13

a new batch in the lab. Until then, I only want to use them in an emergency." He cleaned the head wound and put his supplies back in the cupboard.

Standing up, Tanner quietly walked over to his grandfather and gently put a hand on his shoulder.

"I miss her too, but we scoured that mountain and could find no sign of life. Grandma's gone."

"Maybe we missed something. Maybe she's proof." Merlin nodded toward the unconscious form on the cot, lifting shining, hopeful eyes to Tanner. Tanner turned away, not wanting to feel hope, because it always seemed to turn into despair. He'd seen enough of that.

Not wanting to destroy that glimmer of hope in his grandfather's eyes, Tanner nodded toward the girl. "When, or if she regains consciousness, we will find out where she comes from. Now, I have things to do outside. Let me know if anything changes."

"Of course."

Tweeny glanced up at Tanner as he walked by, headed toward an outcropping of rocks beside the cabin. Seeing the look on Tanner's face, Tweeny said nothing. Glaring, Tanner grabbed the ax, retrieved a large piece of wood from a pile beside the rocks, put it on the flat tree stump and brought the ax down hard. The wood splintered in two.

He repeated it again and again until he had a nice pile of wood for burning. Wiping his brow, he glanced at the sky. It was nearing sunset and they would need to get a good fire going. The dark was too dangerous. Through narrowed

14

eyes, he looked at Tweeny, calmly sitting on a log, sharpening his bowie knife.

"I saw no water when I was at the top of the incline."

"It is advancing very slowly, but it is advancing," answered Tweeny, not looking up.

"I was afraid of that." Tanner's expression turned grim. He stared at Tweeny for a few seconds. He couldn't ask him to get closer. It was too dangerous. If a rover ended up stranded alone after dark, he would need a secure place to spend the night. At times they were hard to find.

Tweeny slid his knife into the sheath. "I will call the guards in. Darkness approaches."

Tweeny chirped twice and soon three shadows came out of the woods. Tanner recognized Raini and Jom, their youngest guards at seventeen. Jesse, newly trained, brought up the rear. They grinned when they saw Tanner. He smiled back and his thoughts traveled to the difficult times when Raini and Jom were born.

It had been only three years after the destruction. The world was a terrifying place. When he held them in his arms, he had cried for the last time. Their mother had died giving birth to them, twins, a boy and a girl. He swore he would never cry again after that and he hadn't, even through the most desolate and heart wrenching times.

Their mother's bleeding had been unstoppable. When she realized she was dying, she had made him promise to look after her newborn babies. She had begged and pleaded. Although only twelve at the time, he had sworn he would take care of them.

Believing his sincerity, she held both babies in her arms, tears trickling down her face and began singing a lullaby. She died before she finished the song and Tanner stood helplessly by watching, his grandfather shaking his head, unable to keep her alive. He had kept his promise, though, and Raini and Jom were like a sister and a brother to him.

Jom, with curly red hair and bright blue eyes greeted Tanner with his usual enthusiasm. "Hi Tan. What's up? You were tearing through here so fast I thought you were going to start a fire."

"Well, I was in a hurry. I found someone on the old trail by the incline. More alive than dead for a change."

Raini, so different from her twin brother, with dark hair and brown eyes, regarded him thoughtfully. "Will he live?"

"She. I don't know. She hit her head pretty hard. With a head injury…" Tanner shrugged.

"What has been going on around here?" He glanced at the twins as he piled fresh wood in the blackened campfire pit, added some small sticks and dried grass, and lit a match A small flame soon begin to flicker.

"It has been quiet," answered Jom, sitting next to Tweeny. He took out his knife and Tweeny nodded, putting his own away and grabbing Jom's.

"Raini was able to bring down a deer earlier and cook is preparing a stew," Jesse added. "I hope it's almost ready because I am starved." As if to punctuate the need for food, his stomach growled.

Tanner leaned back against a large flat rock by the campfire, gazing into the flickering flames. The dry wood was catching on and sparks from the fire were rising and disappearing into the darkening sky above them.

No one said anything as they stared into the flames, each one keeping his own thoughts close. The only sound was Tweeny sharpening Jom's knife against his stone. A muffled bell gonged signaling dinnertime. Jom, Raini, and Jess jumped up and headed toward the cabin.

"Here," said Tweeny, as he held out Jom's sharpened knife.

"Thanks," Jom grabbed it and put it in its sheath attached to his side.

"I'll get you some food and bring it back," Tweeny said, rising and heading toward the cabin. Inside the door, he nearly ran into Jom and Raini who had stopped suddenly, peering with open curiosity at the unconscious female on the cot in the corner of the cabin. Jesse had continued on to the side of the kitchen, too hungry to stop. Merlin, sitting next to her, raised a hand in greeting.

"Go on, get some food. I'm going to stay here and keep a watch on her."

"I'll get some food for you, too," Tweeny said.

"Thanks. I take it Tanner is manning the fire." Tweeny nodded.

Merlin watched as Jesse pushed a lever behind the shelf on the sidewall of the kitchen and the whole shelving unit along the wall swung in revealing a hidden doorway. Beyond was a large cavern with three tunnels leading off in different directions. They disappeared into the cavern and

17

headed toward the right hand tunnel leading to the kitchen and dining area. Tweeny pulled on a lever attached to the backside of the shelves and the hidden door swung closed. Merlin was once again sitting in a simple two-room cabin.

To anyone just happening by, it was a small cabin on the side of the mountain. Before the destruction, Merlin had labored for years, creating a livable environment out of the labyrinth of tunnels and caverns he had discovered on his land.

It had once been a silver mine in the 1800's but once the vein had petered out, it had been abandoned. He had reinforced the inside with wood and steal support until he was sure it was secure with little chance of a cave-in. The cabin was built as a front to hide it.

He had kept his work hidden to everyone but his family and a few close friends, whom he trusted unconditionally. They had helped him through the years bringing in supplies, creating a ventilation system and discovering a power source that would power the whole network with out needing outside utilities.

He had been preparing for an apocalypse he hoped would never happen. For years, he had gathered anything he thought beneficial for a self-sufficient bomb shelter. In the end, his preparedness had saved many lives and most of his family. They had remained inside, safe from the terror and destruction of the aftermath, not knowing at the time when it would be safe to go outside again.

Merlin looked out the window at the encroaching darkness, his features carved with a sadness of loss. Sighing softly, his concerned gaze flickered over to his unconscious patient. He thought of his wife, lost these twenty years, and without thought gently grasped Elizabeth's hand, softly squeezing and saying a prayer to a God he no longer believed in.

Chapter Three

Her eyes reluctantly opened as exhaustion tried to keep them shut. It was dark, very dark and quiet. She tried to shift into a more comfortable position, but the movement sent a bolt of fire through her head. Pain cursed through her body. She sank back into the pillow and wondered where she was. A quiet snore from another room alerted her to another's presence.

Her thoughts were jumbled and her body beaten. She ached everywhere, especially her head and arm. Slowly raising her right arm, she winced at the searing pain in her forearm. Lowering her arm, the pain slowly settled into a burning throb. Aching and uncomfortable, but exhausted beyond measure, she sank back into a deep sleep.

Hours later, the morning sun blazed in the eastern sky and the breeze blowing through the open window began to warm Merlin's face. Gazing outside at the pine trees swaying with the rhythm of the wind, Merlin heard a movement from the bedroom where he had moved his patient last night. Walking quickly to the doorway, he saw Elizabeth trying to open her eyes then gasp in shock and pain. He quickly went to her side.

Merlin touched her hand softly, saying quietly, "It's alright. You're safe."

"Please, the light, it's burning my eyes."

Merlin recoiled as if slapped. No, it's not possible. She can't be a night stalker. She looks too vulnerable, too...soft. And the night stalkers were neither. But they were unable to tolerate the light of the sun; they only came out in the darkness.

The rumor was a later nuclear blast had affected their eyes somehow, making it impossible for them to go out during the day and they had survived by joining together in small bands and stalking at night. They were not kind; in today's harsh world, they took what they could no matter the cost.

Backing away slightly, Merlin cautiously asked, "Who are you?"

Eyes tightly closed, she stiffened and said nothing.

Merlin asked again, "Who are you?" He stepped closer, touching the knife on his side for reassurance.

He gazed at her as her mouth moved, but nothing came out. Finally she whispered hoarsely, "I don't know."

Silence. Merlin didn't move. Her eyes remained tightly closed, confusion and fear written on her features. In the past, they killed night stalkers upon contact. Night stalkers stole humans and they were never seen again. People feared they took humans for food, but no one really knew.

21

He pulled his knife from its sheath, ready to walk over and plunge it into her heart. Many in his small community had died or disappeared from the cruel night stalkers. He knew what he had to do yet he hesitated.

"Please, can you draw the curtains? It's too bright."

Merlin considered her question. Slowly, he closed the curtains in the two windows in the front room and shut the wooden barriers positioned across the windows at night for protection. He then closed the door to the other room and the light in the cabin dimmed considerably, with a little light coming in through cracks.

He stood beside the bed, knife in hand, watching her reaction. She slowly, very slowly opened her eyes. Big green eyes stared up fearfully at him, glanced at the knife in surprise and then with dawning horror.

Merlin very slowly eased the knife back into his sheath and smiled. A night stalker would not be able to tolerate even the small amount of light coming through the cracks and her eyes were green not the discolored yellow of a night stalker.

Elizabeth sighed in relief. Her voice shaking, she quietly asked. "Did I just pass some kind of test?"

"As a matter of fact, you did," Merlin reassured her as he pointed to the water glass on the table by her bed. "Please, drink."

Elizabeth smiled her thanks as she reached for the glass. The water was cool and refreshing on her parched throat. She drank it all.

"I am pleased to make your acquaintance. My name is Marvin Lane. I am the resident doctor here. I would shake your hand, but your right arm has a pretty severe cut on it."

"Pleased to meet you Doctor Lane." She glanced at the knife. "I think."

"Call me Merlin. Everyone does and I'm sorry about the knife." Clearing his throat, he continued, "Now then, have I got this correct? You've lost your memory and have no recollection of who you are?"

"That seems to be the way of it," she quietly responded, her expression grim. Her mind seemed to be a total blank with no comforting memories. Where was she? Who was she? How did she get here? So many questions and she had no answers.

A frown furrowed her brow. "I don't know my name or much of anything else." A combination of fear and helplessness crawled its way under her skin.

"Elizabeth."

"What did you say?" she asked cautiously.

"Your name, it appears to be Elizabeth. If this is yours." Merlin pulled out the nametag from his pocket and showed her. "Does this look familiar?"

Elizabeth shook her head. Merlin handed it to her and she grabbed it with her left hand and looked closely at the name, turning it over in her hand. "No, not familiar at all and that name, it means nothing to me."

"You seem to have a pretty good sized bump on your head. Your loss of memory is probably related to that. Fortunately, it could be temporary."

"Could be? What if it's not?"

"I guess you could think of it as being reborn to a whole new life."

"I don't want a whole new life. I want my old life back. At least I think I do. I don't even know what kind of life I had or what kind of world I live in." At these words, Merlin's face became solemn as he looked away.

A new kind of fear rattled her. "What kind of world do I live in? Why am I here?"

Merlin hesitated. "Well, as to your first question that may take awhile to explain. As to why you are here, my grandson found you on an old hiking trail on the other side of the mountain. Besides this nametag, we really don't know much more than you apparently know."

Elizabeth let that sink in. "You don't know who I am, and I am drawing a blank. What about…?

Suddenly behind Merlin the shelves along the wall seemed to swing in and a doorway appeared. Startled, Elizabeth could only stare.

A dark haired man, early thirties she would guess, walked through the new doorway and pushed the shelves back in place. He was just there, suddenly, silent and powerful, coming toward her before she knew it. Handsome in a rough way, the harsh lines of his face were apparent even in the dim light. Merlin glanced at their new arrival but showed no sign of surprise.

Stopping a few feet from her bedside, showing a flicker of irritation in his dark brown eyes, he glanced at Merlin, "I see your patient has awakened."

"Yes, we were just having a chat, until you barged in. It's okay dear, this is my grandson Tanner Lane."

24

Her mind seemed to splinter just a fraction. A voice forced its way through, "find Tanner and"... a beat of silence... She'd lost the moment and trying to force it didn't work. It just made her head hurt.

Merlin looked at her with concern, "Are you alright?"

"Yes, yes, I thought I remembered something, but it's gone. There's nothing now."

"What was it?"

"A voice." She didn't want them to think she was half mad. "A voice telling me to find something, then it was gone."

Eyes narrowing to something just short of a glare, Tanner regarded her silently. Elizabeth found the only way to hide her nervousness was to let her eyes wander over the cabin. The cabin was sparsely but comfortably furnished. Beside the doorway and each of the two windows were propped rifles. Her eyes widened and a sense of dread tightened her gut. Once again the fear of the unknown began to overwhelm her.

Tanner followed her gaze but said nothing. Merlin stepped closer. "Would you care for something to eat or drink?" She nodded her head, grateful for the diversion.

"Yes, some more water would be wonderful. I'm not really hungry right now." Tanner walked over to the sink by the door and poured her a cup of water, then after sitting it on the nightstand beside the bed, walked toward the door and motioned Merlin to go outside with him.

After the door had closed shut, she sighed, lifting her head a little, and drank some of the water. The coolness of the water felt heavenly on her dry throat, like a cool caress on a fevered brow. She set the glass down and sank back into the pillow, wondering just who she was.

Chapter Four

Walking past the campfire pit to the edge of the trees, Tanner turned around, frowning at Merlin. "How much should we tell her? We don't know who she is or where she came from. Her lost memory seems pretty convenient."

"I believe her," answered Merlin. "She seems truly confused and scared. I don't think it's an act."

"We don't know what other groups and bands of people are doing. I know not all are friendly and content to just barter. Some may want what we have. Keeping our real situation a secret has kept us safe so far."

"That's true, but…"

"What if a strong colony has sent her to find out our strengths and weaknesses? In a week or two she could disappear, report back and we could be attacked and destroyed or taken captive."

"I have a gut feeling she can be trusted. You trust no one."

"Yes, and it's kept us safe. This lost memory thing is a good way to get information from us. I should have never come through the door from the hidden caves. I could have used the other entrance and come through the front door of the cabin. She now knows there is more to this cabin than it seems."

Merlin seemed preoccupied, an odd expression on his face, "The sunlight hurts her eyes."

"What?"

"When she first woke up, she said the sunlight hurt her eyes. I had my knife out and I was ready to…" Merlin's voice broke.

Tanner patted his shoulder. "It's okay. You didn't."

"I know, but I'm a doctor. I save lives. I don't take them."

"It's a different world." Tanner's face was grim. "Someday you may have no choice." Merlin only shook his head.

"As for now, we will just tell her general information about the world, nothing specifically about us. Okay?" Merlin nodded.

He turned and walked back to the cabin, Merlin following. Once inside, they heard gentle snoring. Elizabeth was sound asleep.

Quietly, Tanner spoke to Merlin. "I am going to tell the others to use the side entrance for the time being. I don't want anyone else coming from the caves through here." With that he pushed a hidden lever behind the shelf and disappeared into the dim interior, the door closing quietly behind him.

Merlin sat at the kitchen table by the sink lost in thought. When he had reinforced the tunnels and caverns of the old mine, he'd found a small winding tunnel that had wound itself back to within a half-mile from the cabin. He figured it would make a good second entrance and exit to the caves. It would lessen the risk of anyone becoming trapped inside with no way out.

He had camouflaged it so it looked like the surrounding rock and, with two hidden cameras facing outward, outside surveillance was easy. Most of their people used it, only occasionally using the cabin entrance.

Inside the tunnels were "his people." Friends and family who had made it in time and later people who had survived the holocaust and were accepted into what he thought of as a new settlement, which they had named the Manitou Colony, after the nearby town.

The small tourist town of Manitou Springs was located just west of Colorado Springs in the mountains. The cabin sat on the far side of the mountain southeast of the town and above it. The town had weathered the initial destruction fairly well, but through the years, parts of the small town had gradually swept away in flood after flood from the river that cut through the town. High enough above the river, the cabin had survived the deluges.

The first two years of the aftermath had been the worse. Due to the debris and fall out in the atmosphere, they were forced to stay inside the converted mine. At first, there was still communication coming in from the outside world. Though it was bad, people had been assured that "we were winning the battle," although in the beginning, many major cities had been bombed and laid waste. Later, planes had flown over Colorado Springs and leveled it. The Cheyenne Mountain Military Installation had supposedly been destroyed.

The lunar fiasco had started it all and no one really knew who pushed the first buttons or dropped the first bombs. Of course, the United Stated government had retaliated. They had wiped North Korea off the map and leveled any Eastern country they considered a threat. When the smoke cleared, all communication had ceased. The grids had been wiped out or severely damaged and most of the satellites destroyed or impaired.

Then came the cold. The climate change, due to all the debris in the atmosphere, darkened the sky, making weather conditions wintry and frigid. The cameras to the outside world told a partial story of what happened.

The norm became dark skies everyday, with occasional clearing. The temperature rarely got above 50 degrees and usually hovered around freezing. Constant dark snow was falling and the world was made unrecognizable and bleak in the aftermath of the inconceivable and unimaginable destruction and waste. Who had won? Did it matter now?

After about a year, when Merlin looked at the outside world through his camera, he noticed a brighter sky and it lasted throughout most of the day. Gradually the skies cleared. Checking radiation levels weekly, they waited another six months. Although, the levels had never been that high in the surrounding area, Merlin thought it safer to be cautious and finally he opened the cabin door to the outside world.

When he breathed in the air, it was fresh, as if the world had renewed itself. Then he realized, there had probably been no pollution being released into the air daily since the holocaust. No cars, no industry, nothing to pollute the air. The radiation level was also very low.

There was still a chill, but as the weeks went by, the temperature slowly began to increase. The pine trees, furs and spruces had weathered the cold and dwindling sunlight. Plants began to spring forth, as if they had been in hibernation. Many animals had somehow survived and were spied foraging for food.

Considering it now safe, Merlin and Tanner had decided to explore the area to see for themselves the results of the destruction. Manitou Springs had survived the initial devastation. Walking through the remains of the small town, there had been no sign of life, or traffic or even tire treads. Before, at this time of day, there would be tourists wandering up and down the main street, an assortment of shops open for business, and the owner's dogs languishing in front of the shops.

Some buildings were still intact but in disrepair, with doors ajar and windows broken. Most had long ago been looted for anything of value. The streets were piled with garbage, dirt and dead bodies, human and animal. Some had been picked over by hungry animals, most decomposed beyond recognition.

As they cautiously walked through, it seemed like a ghost town. Their footsteps echoed on the wooden walkways. No sign of life besides the occasional stray animal salvaging for food or finding shelter in the buildings.

Heading to the northern part of the town, they decided to take the incline to the top of the mountain for a view of Colorado Springs. They easily found the steps and they were surprisingly intact. The two of them climbed the steps in silence, the mood gloomy. Reaching the top, nothing could have prepared them for what they saw. They gazed at the incomprehensible scene below them; a city once teaming with life was now in utter ruin.

Merlin remembered how they had stood there in shock, hugging one another and then staring in disbelief at what had once been their home but was now a city shattered, demolished beyond recognition. Most the buildings had been leveled to rubble and the few still standing looked like grey tomb stones jutting into the sky.

Everything seemed to be shrouded in dust and debris. The earth appeared blackened in areas and the roads and highways were smashed and cracked like someone had lost control of a wrecking ball. All they could do was stare in helpless dismay at the unimaginable sight before their eyes.

They had stayed awhile, quietly talking and sharing the binoculars, looking for signs of life. It was a dismal replica of the smaller town they had just walked through, only on a grander scale of devastation.

Returning home, the mood had been somber, but they were glad to be alive amidst so much death. They had reported back what they had seen. To keep disease down, they had returned with the help of the others in the colony and piled the bodies in the center of town and burned them.

No burial or last rites, just the stench of burning flesh and rotting carcasses. The reality of their situation was apparent. Their world was irretrievably damaged, changed beyond anything imaginable.

Merlin realized at the time that the most difficult challenge facing them would be their ability to survive in an environment that no longer followed the same rules as before. They had no idea what they would find "out there." Now a new and perilous world awaited, a world they had unwittingly inherited.

Chapter Five

She awakened with the sensation of being watched. Merlin was sitting in front of the window his head tilted thoughtfully, his gaze focused elsewhere. Elizabeth berated herself for her anxiety. Then a shadow disengaged itself from the corner. Flinching in fear, Elizabeth let out a startled gasp. Hearing the noise, Merlin shook himself out of his thoughts and turned in concern toward Elizabeth.

Upon seeing who had frightened her, Merlin chuckled, "Tweeny, quit scaring my patient."

"Sorry, Doc. I thought she was sleeping," Tweeny smiled shyly at Elizabeth.

"Elizabeth, this is Tweeny the rover. He is part of our little community here."

"Forgive me," Elizabeth murmured, embarrassed at her jumpiness. "You startled me."

"I do that sometimes. I'm pretty sneaky and I'm always catching someone off guard." Small and wiry with light brown hair streaked with gray flowing down to his shoulders, he had the facial appearance of a mischievous elf with a glimmer in his eye and a disarming grin. Elizabeth couldn't help but smile back.

"Pleased to meet you, Tweeny the sneaky rover. Um, what is a rover?"

Tweeny glanced at Merlin who shrugged.

"A rover, well a rover roves."

"Oh, you mean move about, check things out?"

"Yes, it's my job."

"Oh, I see."

"We all have jobs here, usually something we're good at and I'm good at roving," Tweeny said with pride.

Clearing his throat at the door, Tanner walked inside, frowning in irritation "What do we have here, a little 'let's get acquainted' tea party?"

"Actually, a little tea would be nice," Tweeny replied. Tanner glared at him.   "Um, I was just leaving. Nice to meet you Elizabeth." Tweeny disappeared outside.

Looking at Merlin, Tanner gestured in her direction. "I wanted to ask her a few questions."

"Your interrogation will have to wait," Merlin replied. "She is still too weak. Maybe tomorrow."

Tanner gave a curt nod, glanced at Elizabeth and grumbling under his breath, strode back outside and disappeared around the side of the cabin.

"Is he always so grumpy?" Elizabeth, carefully rising to her elbows, asked Merlin.

"Actually, that was his good mood," Merlin quipped. "Are you hungry?"

"Yes I am and some tea would be nice if you have it." Rising up to a sitting position, she glanced around the room. Elizabeth was glad Merlin had drawn the curtains, keeping the room dim. The light still bothered her eyes. She felt a dull ache in her head and her arm still throbbed from the deep cut. "I'm feeling much better, although my head still hurts... and my arm."

"I can give you something for the pain." Merlin walked over to her bedside, "Do you need some help?"

"Yes, thank you. I need... uh...I need a relieving station."

"What?" Merlin looked confused, then nodded with understanding. "Oh, you mean a bathroom?"

"No, I don't need a bath right now, maybe later. I need a room with a toilet."

"That's what we call a bathroom." Merlin looked at her curiously, an odd expression on his face. "Let me help you. It's through the bedroom. That door over there." He pointed toward the other room.

Merlin helped her walk to the bathroom, letting her lean on him, her legs a little wobbly. She closed the door behind her and noticed the mirror above a sink. With apprehension, she looked in the mirror. Relief swept through her.

She knew herself; her eyes, mouth, nose all seemed familiar. It was comforting although she still had no memory. At least her face seemed her own and not that of a stranger. She closed her eyes and slowly let out a shuttering breath, a coil of tension loosening itself from around her spine.

Merlin had a cup of hot tea waiting when she cautiously walked past her bed to the kitchen area. Her legs felt stronger. Carefully sitting at the table, she grabbed the mug and inhaled the spicy, pungent aroma. "Smells good. It smells like cinnamon."

"Yes, it's spicy chamomile," Merlin smiled. "Well, it looks like you still remember some things. That's not surprising. Many people who lose their memories still retain basic knowledge and usually know how to perform their jobs at work, read, do complex math and are perfectly normal besides not remembering anything about their own personal lives."

Merlin sat down at the table. "With a hit on the head, you may find your memories return slowly and in bits and pieces. It might be confusing until you regain enough of your memories to make sense out of it all. Or everything may all come back at once, though that is more unusual."

"It is a little disconcerting," Elizabeth sighed. "Just now, I looked in the mirror and saw a face I knew well. That was a relief, but it didn't jolt back any memories."

"In good time my dear." Merlin patted her hand.

"I know. When I try to force it, it just makes my head hurt." Elizabeth sipped the strong, fragrant tea, savoring the taste. A knock sounded in a cupboard by the bookcase.

"Ah, breakfast," Merlin smiled. He walked to the cupboard, opened it and pulled out a plate of eggs and toast. "I hope you like this."

Elizabeth's mouth watered as he placed the plate on the small table. She needed no prompting. The food smelled and tasted delicious. She literally couldn't remember when she'd eaten food this good.

After eating it all, she pushed her plate back and sighed in contentment. "Excuse my table manners. I didn't realize I was so hungry."

"Well, you were unconscious for two days until you woke up this morning, then you slept all day. Now it is late afternoon, so it's no wonder you were so hungry."

"Oh, I didn't realize I was out so long." She looked down at her nightdress. Surely, you didn't find me in this?"

"No, no. I put your clothes in the dresser in the bedroom. Molly helped me get you changed. She does all the cleaning around here." He looked around the cabin and glanced uncomfortably at the bookcase.

Elizabeth set her teacup down and said in a hushed voice, "It's okay. I won't ask you any questions you can't answer."

"Thank you," Merlin hesitated. In a quiet solemn voice he said, "Elizabeth I'm sorry." A hint of sadness clouded his expression.

"Pardon?"

"About this morning, the knife and all."

"I'm sure you had your reasons."

"Uh…About that. Do you know of the night stalkers?" He watched her reaction carefully. She shook her head; not a flicker of emotion crossed her face.

"I have no recollection of them."

"Okay. Well, they are humans, but they're not normal." He decided it would be best to speak bluntly. "You see the world has changed. Humans now live in a world that was almost destroyed by catastrophe and war. The night stalkers were some how affected by the radiation and they are blinded by the sunlight. They only come out at night."

"I see," Elizabeth replied. "So, my initial reaction to the sunlight caused you to believe I may be one of these night stalkers."

"Why, yes." Before she could respond, he hurried on. "You see we have had run-ins with them. At night they would attack our settlement here, capturing our people. We don't know why or where the night stalkers take them. They just disappear. It began about five years ago. We are now prepared for them. We have flood lights and the wolves warn us and no one goes out alone after dark."

"Wolves?"

"Yes. They guard the encampment. About three years ago, we saw two wolves around this area. We let them alone and they did the same. One day, Tanner had extra meat and he threw it near their home by the cabin. Then he brought a piece of clothing from everyone in the colony and laid each one out near by and collected the clothing the next day.

Gradually, we formed an unspoken alliance. They never attack anyone from the colony, but if a stranger approaches, they bark and howl to get our attention. They hate night stalkers and will warn us if any are close by."

Glancing at Elizabeth's surprised look, Merlin continued, "We put your shirt out yesterday. Tanner picked it up earlier and Molly's washing it. You see, they have our scents as friends not foes, but unfortunately, they pee all over the clothes. It's there way of helping us, but still marking their boundaries."

Elizabeth looked at Merlin in disbelief. "If that's what it takes for a little protection around here…" She started laughing. She could hardly contain her mirth and Merlin soon joined her. If felt good to laugh. Slowly, their chuckles faded, leaving both of them wiping at their eyes in silence.

Standing outside the cabin, Tanner heard their laughter. It had been a long time since he heard such joyful abandon. He wanted to join them and share in it, but he hesitated, feeling like an outsider. When their laughter subsided, he stepped into the cabin.

Chapter Six

Merlin greeted Tanner. "I was just telling Elizabeth about the night stalkers."

"I didn't realize it was such a humorous topic," Tanner muttered.

"Huh? Oh...no, I was telling Elizabeth about the wolves and how they mark their territory."

"By the way, here's your shirt." Tanner laid it on the table.

Picking it up, she smelled it, and gave in to another chuckle she could not contain. Seeing Tanner's frown, she stifled it and looked down at her teacup. "Thank you. Molly did a good job."

"I see you're feeling better," Tanner leaned against the doorframe noticing the empty plate on the table.

Merlin rose to clear the table. "Yes, she is and she ate a hearty breakfast. I was explaining some things to Elizabeth, trying to gauge how much she knows about the world we live in."

"I know the world is different now and I am going to read Merlin's account of the aftermath to better understand,"

Elizabeth held up Merlin's journal. "I do know the year is 2041." She was pleased with remembering that.

Tanner and Merlin glanced at each other.

"Well, it is isn't it?" She was feeling a little uncomfortable now.

"Here in this settlement we have started over, from the beginning of…the beginning of… these new times," Tanner said hesitantly. "To keep it simple, the year is 20."

"20?"

"Twenty years into the aftermath," Merlin replied. "It's been twenty years since…since it began. And that was roughly the middle of September. We picked September 22nd as the beginning of each New Year. You know, the fall equinox and all. Although, now with the earth…"

"Merlin, can I speak to you a moment," Tanner interrupted.

The earth. Elizabeth sat there in deep thought. Of course, the earth and earth's satellite…the planets. I study the solar system. There is something important about that. She lost the thought. She tried to concentrate, but her head began pounding from the effort.

Slowly rising to her feet, she walked over to the bookcase. She knew she liked to read. Glancing at the titles, she found one that looked interesting. Easing down in an over-stuffed chair by the bookcase, she began thumbing through it.

"We've got a problem," muttered Tanner as he faced Merlin beside the burned out campfire. "Tweeny says Dwight McGee has left the Academy Colony. He took a few people who were willing to go with him and they're now

40

camped out by the river close to the old burned out small pox settlement."

"Why would he leave the Academy? They have been doing real well from what I've heard. They're growing crops and are producing their own energy."

"The old colonel died last month."

"Yes, I knew him, a good man. Because of his leadership skills, the academy has really prospered in the last ten years."

Tanner nodded. "It seems there was some bickering as to who should take command. Most wanted Mitch Evans to run things, but a small group was behind Dwight McGee, the colonel's son."

"From what I've heard, he's a hot head."

"When the colonel was alive, he kept him under control," replied Tanner. "Now, McGee thinks he's the new colonel, a family hierarchal thing. When the majority voted in Mitch as the new leader of the colony, McGee was furious. He threatened Mitch and some others. They told him to leave. He did."

"That's good."

"The problem is, he cleaned out most of their firearms and ammunition. He got enough men backing him that Mitch is worried he might cause trouble with the settlements. McGee knows the water is approaching and he'll be looking for higher ground."

"The Academy is not much higher than where he is camped by the river." He met Tanner's gaze and stiffened, understanding dawning.

Tanner nodded. "We're at 7000 feet. If he's looking for greener pastures, he'll come here. Tomorrow, I am going with Tweeny and Shelton to McGee's settlement by the river and do some investigating."

"Well, be careful," Merlin warned.

"We're not going to exactly announce ourselves." Tanner laughed, but there was little humor in it. Merlin grabbed Tanner by the arm, as he turned to go back inside, halting the younger man.

"I know you want to find out who she is and where she comes from, but go easy on her. She is still recovering from her injuries and confused. What if you suddenly had no memories, no history of who you were?"

Tanner sighed. "I know. But, if we are going to accept her into the colony, we need to know something about her. What if another colony sent her to spy on us to get inside information? It's not unheard of. Maybe she's working for McGee. It's kind of a coincidence that she shows up right after they break from the main colony."

"It could be just that, a coincidence," Merlin replied.

"Look, I'll go easy on her. It's not the inquisition after all." Satisfied, Merlin turned to head over to the other entrance. Tanner gazed after Merlin till he lost sight of him and then stood in the dappled rays of the sun, lost in his thoughts.

Twenty minutes later, Tanner quietly stepped into the cabin and slowly closed the door. Totally absorbed in a book on her lap, Elizabeth didn't hear him come in. He stood watching her for a moment and finally cleared his throat. She jumped in surprise.

42

"Sorry, didn't mean to scare you."

"Oh. That's…I'm fine," Elizabeth stammered." With a guilty expression on her face, she rose and quickly put the book back in the bookcase.

"What are you reading?"

"Oh, I didn't notice the title. Just something I picked up. I've been glancing through a few books. Quite the library here."

"Yes, grandfather prepared well." They stared at each other for a moment.

"Well, I'm tired. I think I will rest awhile."

Seeing her discomfort and weary expression, Tanner decided he would wait to question her, "Merlin says you need some privacy. You can use the bedroom." He pointed toward the other room. "It will be yours for now."

"Oh, thank you." Elizabeth smiled slightly, closing the book and putting it back on the shelf. She reached toward another book. "I think I'll take this book of poems to read." Brushing past him, she grabbed her shirt off the table and stepped into the bedroom, closing the door behind her.

Tanner strolled over to the bookcase and plucked the book off the shelf she had been reading when he walked in. His gaze flew to the closed door then back to the title: Relativistic Astrophysics and Cosmology. She wasn't just glancing at this book; she was totally absorbed in it. He wondered and not for the first time just who in the hell this strange woman was.

After a few moments, Elizabeth heard Tanner quietly go out the front door. She breathed a sigh of relief, not really knowing why she became so nervous around him and why she was so reluctant to tell him what she was reading.

The big question in her mind, why was she able to understand that book so easily? From what she had gathered talking to Merlin, knowing how to survive in a dangerous world seemed more essential than knowledge of astrophysics. That kind of knowledge didn't seem very practical in today's world.

She wondered if other colonies were more advanced in the sciences. Maybe she had received the education from some unknown settlement. And what was she doing unconscious on that trail? So many questions; her head was pounding. She noticed a glass of water on the nightstand by the bed and two pills with a note. *Take these for the pain, Merlin.* She did and then lay down.

It was becoming too much for Elizabeth to absorb everything. Her thoughts whirled around in her head until she felt like she was drowning in uncertainty. Unease tying a deep knot in her belly, she fought to remember something, anything. Finally, exhaustion overwhelmed her and she fell into a dreamless sleep.

Chapter Seven

"You are much improved, my dear. How are you feeling?" Sitting at the table in the kitchen, Elizabeth glanced at Merlin as he completed his examination of her head and arm.

"Better. My head only hurts when I try to remember something." She handed Merlin his journal. "Thank you for letting me read that. I...I don't know what to say. You have survived when so many perished. I'm so sorry for your losses."

Unable to keep the sadness from his expression, he nodded. "It's been twenty years since I've seen my wife, but I still think of her every day." With a sigh, he rose to his feet and crossed the floor to the small desk in the corner. He tucked the journal safely in the top drawer, closed it gently and walked back to the table.

"She was in the Cheyenne Mountain military facility when it was destroyed. I thought she would get out in time, but…"

Elizabeth grabbed his hand and squeezed. Merlin welcomed the sympathetic gesture and seemed to come to a decision. "I think you need to see more of our home here."

Elizabeth stiffened. "I'm not ready to go outside." The outdoors frightened her. It was too wide open, too bright and left her feeling vulnerable. Having spent most of the last two days in the bedroom, she realized she was more comfortable in the dimmer light. The sunlight still bothered her eyes.

"No, not outside." Merlin smiled. "Inside. I want to show you the inside of the mountain."

"Oh. I had the feeling that Tanner didn't want me knowing any more than he deemed I should."

"I am a pretty good judge of character and I trust you. Anyway, Tanner's not here right now."

He quickly stood up and motioned her toward the bookcase, pulled the lever and the door quietly opened. She followed him through and the door silently closed behind them.

Feeling a bit breathless, Elizabeth looked around her in surprise. A shadowy tunnel with dim lights overhead veered off to the right. They strode along that briefly until the tunnel angled off toward a dining hall. The main passageway wound toward the left and out of sight.

"A few years before the catastrophe I began converting this old mine into a livable shelter," Merlin explained. "I knew it was perfect for what I had in mind. It is large enough to hold 100 people comfortably; although there are only eighty-three people in the colony right now, not including you."

"Why did you do it?"

Merlin thought for a moment. "When I found the mine on my land, I knew I had a remarkable opportunity to build a sanctuary that would shelter people if the unthinkable happened. I worked for ten years to get it right, creating an environment that would be able to sustain itself. If things became really bad, anyone not prepared would be vulnerable. I also came to the realization that the only way to be safe in the beginning would be to retreat."

"Retreat?"

"Yes. Disappear into the mountain without a trace. If no one knows you are there, they can't attack you or try to get what you have."

They had stepped into the dining hall. Clusters of tables and chairs were neatly arranged around the room. A long counter stretched across the backside and behind it was the kitchen. There were workers preparing lunch behind the counter.

"I want you to meet someone." Merlin steered her toward the kitchen. "Is Gertie back there, Elsa?" A young girl, who looked to be in her teens smiled and pointed to a doorway.

"She's in the back baking some bread."

Breathing in the wonderful aroma of baking bread, Elizabeth followed Merlin through the doorway. He greeted an older woman who was rolling dough on a large table. "Gertie, I want you to meet Elizabeth here."

"Well, it's about time they brought you down here to meet us," Gertie replied, smiling. She was older with some gray in her hair and a few lines on her round pleasant face. "Lunch will be ready soon. Have you enjoyed the meals we've sent to the cabin?"

"Yes. They have been delicious. Thank you."

"Well, lunch will be ready soon."

"I'm going to show her around. We'll be back." Merlin escorted Elizabeth through the kitchen and toward another doorway.

"Behind the kitchen is our industrial shop where we make things. We have sewing machines, and equipment to makes shoes, backpacks, well, all kinds of items. The laundry room runs along the side."

He pointed to the right toward a doorway. As they walked through the shop, people working at the machines waved and smiled as they passed. Hearing a humming as they stepped through the last doorway, she saw computers, electronic equipment and electrical grids.

"This is our maintenance department and where we are linked in to our power source."

What is your power source?" Elizabeth asked.

"We use the river. It flows through the canyon near here rather forcefully. We convert that energy into the power needed to generate electricity to run everything."

"You're an electrician as well as a doctor?"

"Not really. Jackson, Tanner's father, he did all the wiring. Now we have Will Reece who is the facilities supervisor as well as our computer whiz. I don't see him around just now. I'll introduce you to him later."

"In your journal you said your son and daughter in law..."

"Yes, Jackson and Tanner's mother Jill never made it to safety." Merlin sighed. "They were on their way here when they stopped for gas. Tanner was already here. They had dropped him off the day before. Jill phoned and said they were delayed because of all the traffic. That was the last I heard from them. The moon was struck, debris began raining down on the earth and soon the bombs followed. It all happened so quickly. They didn't have a chance. We boarded up the cabin and went inside. Of course, we kept the cameras on, always watching, hoping they would show up."

Merlin sighed. "Tanner took it pretty hard and he just withdrew. It took him many years to get over it, but when Jom and Raini were born, something happened to him and he seemed to find a purpose to his life again."

"I am so sorry for your loss," murmured Elizabeth.

"Thank you." Walking as far back as they could go into the mountain, Merlin pointed toward another tunnel veering to the left, and Elizabeth found herself in another dimly lit corridor. "This leads to the gardens."

Walking along in the dim light, Elizabeth suddenly stumbled. Taking her arm, Merlin asked if she was all right. Disoriented, Elizabeth frowned with confusion. With reluctance, she met his concerned gaze.

49

"A memory. I think I just had a memory." Abruptly, an image had appeared of a corridor similar to this, yet different. It seemed familiar, as if she had been through it many times. Then, just as abruptly, it was gone.

"What was it?" Merlin asked in concern.

"A corridor, like this, underground. It was as if I was there."

Stopping in the tunnel, Merlin studied her. "Do you feel comfortable here?"

"Yes, more so than in the cabin."

"You may have been living underground. That's why the sunlight is so unbearable and you have a fear of the outside. Being here may be jarring some memories because it is familiar to what you're used to."

"Tanner found me outside. How could I have gotten there?"

"It is indeed a mystery," Merlin shrugged. "Come, we are nearly there." Elizabeth hesitated for a moment looking at the back of Merlin's retreating figure. Gazing around her, she frowned then blinking, tried to remember more. Nothing. She gave up and hurried after Merlin.

Chapter Eight

Merlin went around a bend in the corridor. When she caught up to him she halted in wonder at the unbelievable sight in front of her. Stretching out into a bowl shaped cavern, were plants of all sizes, small fruit trees, berry bushes, patches of vegetables and scented herbs. Above her was a large opening in the rocks and light was streaming down into the cavern. She shielded her eyes and Merlin grabbed a dark pair of glasses on the table at the entrance and handed them to her. Thanking him, she quickly put them on, shielding her eyes from the bright sunshine.

"This is our masterpiece. The top of the mountain caved in long ago. It is so sheer, it would be impossible to climb up the outside and get in that way. The opening is only in this area. At night we have a roof that rolls into place." He pointed to the back of the cavern where a giant steal roof was slanted across the back.

"It took two years to make the roof. We had it closed shut in the beginning of the aftermath. The first year, we lived off canned and dried food. Once we were able to go out again, we opened up the roof and started the garden."

"Of course. I'm sure you had a vast supply of seeds," she quipped. Merlin nodded.

"It's beautiful." Elizabeth took a deep breath of the sweet-scented air, enriched with…animal scents? "Do you have animals here?"

"Follow me," Merlin urged. "We have some small animals, goats for milk, and we have chickens for eggs and for food." He led her through patches of carrots and strawberries to a fenced area. In the back was a small barn with a corral surrounding it and a woman was talking to a girl milking a goat.

52

"Hi Marsha, I want you to meet someone." Merlin yelled. Marsha smiled and walked toward them.

"Hello Merlin." She smiled at Elizabeth. Hi, I'm Marsha Hendricks." She reached out her hand in welcome, and Elizabeth shook it. Marsha looked to be in her forties, physically fit with her brown hair pulled back away from her face. Her smile seemed genuine and Elizabeth liked her immediately.

"Nice to meet you. I'm Elizabeth."

"I'm giving Elizabeth a tour of the facilities. Marsha here is our veterinarian. She made it through the first year on her own and trekked here from Wyoming. She's been with us ever since."

"That must have been quite the hardship to get here."

"Yes, it was." A collie loped over and joined her. "If it wasn't for this guys' mom and dad, I would have never made it."

"When I saw Marsha at the door of the cabin, I couldn't believe my eyes, really. She and the dogs looked pretty haggard." Marsha nodded in agreement, her eyes taking on a haunted looked for a moment.

"You see, she knew about this place, "Merlin continued. "Jill had contacted her before the aftermath. She was concerned with what animals would be most valuable so she phoned Marsha, whom she had met at a survivalist convention."

"I didn't really know if anyone had survived here. The cabin looked deserted from the outside. When there was no response at first, I just lay down in exhaustion, with a little

53

bit of despair thrown in. I knew of no other place to go and in my mind I was done for. You can imagine my surprise when Merlin came running out. I was never so happy to see anyone in my life." She smiled fondly at Merlin.

"We were glad to see you too, and not just because we needed a vet," Merlin joked.

"You would have put me to work doing something. Here, everyone has a job."

Elizabeth thought about that. What kind of work could she do? An astronomer didn't seem very practical in this world.

Marsha, seeing a look of worry on Elizabeth's face said, "Don't worry. You get a say when it comes to job designation. We have found out that it makes things run much smoother when the people here like their jobs." She gave Merlin a telling look.

Merlin shrugged. "Marsha is referring to Stan Crawford. I don't think any job would have worked for him."

At Elizabeth's questioning look, Merlin explained. "We took Stan in about a month ago. He said he had been staying at the Academy Colony, but things didn't work out. Tanner didn't want him inside so we told him all we had to offer was guard duty and he had to sleep outside. He begrudgingly took it."

Bending down to pet Marsha's dog, Merlin continued, "Two weeks ago, Tanner was out front when he heard Elsa screaming. He found her trying to fight off Stan. He had ripped her shirt and thrown her on the ground, intent on raping her. Tanner pulled Stan off and began pummeling him. Tweeny and I had to pull him off or he might have killed him. Tanner literally picked him up and threw him down the hill. The last I saw of him, he was limping off to the east."

Seeing Elizabeth's shocked expression, Merlin tried to reassure her. "Don't worry, we haven't had too many bad ones like that. Tanner weeds them out pretty quickly. Now, let's be on our way. Nice to see you Marsha." Marsha waved, turning back to her work.

Merlin and Elizabeth headed toward the front again. The aromatic scent of herbs lingered in the air. Elizabeth noticed workers tending to the wide variety of plant life in the gardens. When they passed and saw that it was Merlin, they always smiled or waved. Their fondness for Merlin was apparent. In her mind she saw an image of workers looking down with fear in their eyes. She tried to reach for the memory, hold on to it, but the image flickered out before she could grasp it.

Chapter Nine

Merlin pointed ahead. "The lab is up ahead and beyond that is the medical center. That's where I have my office." They approached the bottom of the stone bowl separating the garden from the lab and entered a doorway.

"You can put the sunglasses on the table there," Merlin indicated. "We are back under the mountain again."

A man was bent over a microscope. "Hello, Frank." The man looked up distractedly and returned Merlin's greeting. Two lab assistants, working with slides under a microscope at a nearby table waved.

"I am showing our new arrival around. This is Frank Bartlett." Frank was lanky looking and his hair seemed to be sticking up at odd angles, the stereotype of a geeky professor. "Frank was a chemistry professor at Colorado University in Boulder. We are very fortunate to have him. This is Elizabeth."

"Pleased to meet you." Elizabeth shook his hand. "You have an amazing place in here."

"We certainly do." Frank swiped at his hair, trying to pat it down and adjusted his glasses. "We don't have many guests coming through here, but yes, considering the circumstances, this lab is state of the art. We are able to synthesize chemicals from the garden and outside sources. The pain killers Merlin gave you for your injuries were made here." He waved his arm to encompass the lab.

Elizabeth looked about her in awe. Merlin indicated another doorway. "That is my favorite place. We'll let you get back to work Frank." Frank waved them on, already turning back to his microscope.

They entered the medical center. There were four cots arranged neatly in the main room with a curtain between each cot. Off to the side was a private examining room and an office. A young child was lying on one of the cots sleeping. Beside him, sat a young man in a white jacket.

"Hi, James. How is our young patient doing? By the way, this is Elizabeth. Elizabeth this is my assistant, James and little Toby." Merlin looked fondly at the boy.

James smiled and nodded his head at Elizabeth in greeting. "Toby is resting comfortably." He laid the back of his hand gently on the boy's forehead. "His fever has gone down considerably."

"Excellent." Merlin directed her to a closed door on the other side. He opened the door and motioned her in. "This is our delivery room. Many babies have been born here since the aftermath." Elizabeth looked around her at the homey effects of the wall and the pictures. It was comfortable and soothing. A rocking chair sat in one corner.

"Sadly, we've lost some of the children." Merlin shook his head. "They are our most important treasure." Elizabeth nodded her head in agreement.

"The last section is up ahead." They were back in the main tunnel that led to each of the sections and connected them. "These are our living quarters. We've got individual rooms for one person or a couple and two rooms for families. The rooms are small but comfortable." Merlin directed her to the tunnel that veered off to the right. He pointed to the left. "That takes us to the other exit."

This corridor they entered looked like a college dormitory with doors to the rooms on each side. Merlin opened the first one. In it she saw a small bed, nightstand, and dresser. A soft-looking chair was in the corner. It was very inviting. She glanced at the room in longing.

Merlin studied Elizabeth. "Would you like to stay here now instead…"

"Oh, yes!" Elizabeth interrupted. "Oh, sorry, Merlin. I just feel so much more comfortable in the shelter. The cabin…" She trailed off.

"I understand," Merlin chuckled. "I am beginning to think you feel comfortable here because your home was in a shelter. Maybe, you were rarely outside."

"You could be right." Elizabeth nodded in agreement. "I love this room. It's perfect. That is… if it's available."

"Yes, it's vacant. I will get Molly to bring you some clean clothes from the extra supplies in laundry. Let me show you the rest of this section."

They walked down a long corridor. A few people walked by and greeted them. At the end of the corridor were bathrooms and showers. Then it widened into a recreation area. There were couches, a television and a devise she wasn't sure about. Two people were playing pool at a table in the corner.

"The television is set up to play movies. No one is communicating on it from the outside world. We keep hoping." Merlin pointed to a room past the pool table. "Over there is a workout area. We have weights, some stationary bikes, and a couple of tread mills. You can check it out later. That winding tunnel over there goes down to the bottom of the cave. We have some more living quarters and the rest is a storage facility for supplies and equipment."

They walked through the recreation room. "Behind that wall" Merlin pointed, "is a heated pool for relaxing.

"Where does the water come from?" Elizabeth asked.

"There is an underground spring we tap. That is why the town was called Manitou Springs. People used to drink it right out of fountains on the sidewalk. We also recycle some of the water. We have a water treatment area in maintenance." Merlin glanced at Elizabeth, noticing her fatigue for the first time. "You look tired. Let's get you back to your new room."

On the way back, Merlin exclaimed. "Oh, I forgot something. I think this will interest you."

Going back through the living quarters, they reached the main tunnel and took that toward the other exit. The tunnel veered again to the right. Merlin pointed toward the left and about twenty feet away the tunnel widened then came to a dead end into a solid looking door with a man sitting beside it.

"There's the other exit." Merlin waved at the man. "Hello Sam. Pretty quiet over here?"

"Very quiet. Had a raccoon digging around outside, but he took off when he couldn't find any food." Sam chuckled.

"This is Elizabeth. She's going to be living with us." Sam waved. "That's Sam. He is one of the exit guards."

They went a few feet down the right corridor, veering away from the exit. Suddenly, Elizabeth found herself in a large cavern with rows and rows of books.

"This is our library," Merlin said proudly. "There are a plethora of books about nearly every subject imaginable." Elizabeth could only stare in wonder.

"I began collecting books years ago. Without a doubt, the instructional manuals have come in handy. You can check out any book you want to read. We have everything from Shakespeare to Darwin. Just write down the title beside your name on the checkout record book we keep over there on that shelf. When you bring it back, cross off the title and your name."

"That sounds easy enough." Elizabeth said as she gazed around the room. "I'm sure I will spend time in here."

"There are some comfy chairs and pillows scattered around if you find the atmosphere in here to your liking."

"Thank you. I am going to make myself at home in my new room after I find some books of interest." She began browsing through the bookshelves.

"Do you want some lunch, Elizabeth?"

"After I rest."

"I will tell Gertie to save a plate for you."

Elizabeth nodded and Merlin turned to go. "Oh by the way, maybe you can figure out something about yourself by the books you're interested in. See you soon." Merlin waved and left.

"Hmmm, maybe I can. Where should I begin?" she wondered aloud.

Before she began her search, she walked over to the record book of checked out items. She was thinking of Merlin's last comment and found herself curious about something. What type of books, if any, did Tanner enjoy reading?

As she turned the pages of the record book, she saw his name and the books he had recently checked out. She smiled slightly, scratching her head, and looked again, making sure she had read the titles correctly. It seemed odd. She knew with certainty that she had read these books, yet she knew nothing of certainty about herself. The oddest part was that Tanner had also read them. Looking at the titles, she realized he was not at all what he seemed.

"Well this is certainly illuminating." She closed the record book as a breath of laughter escaped her.

Chapter Ten

Tanner crouched low behind a charred wall. He could hear approaching voices of two people walking away from their campsite by the river. Glancing behind him quickly, he saw Tweeny and Shelton cautiously taking cover. The three had been waiting for nightfall to get closer to McGee's camp. The sun was just setting and their goal was to eavesdrop on any conversation concerning McGee's plans. Outnumbered, Tanner wanted to get in and out as quickly as possible.

Two men strode into sight. Tanner cursed under his breath. He recognized one of the men, Crawford.

"I tell you, there's women up there, healthy women." Crawford said, stopping within feet of Tanner's position. "Not like the scraggily ones at camp who don't fight back anymore." He snickered. Tanner wanted to punch him.

"McGee says we need more man power," his companion frowned, stopping and looking around at the burned out campsite. "He's in charge around here and what he says is the law. You're new, so my advice to you, don't get pushy. Do you know what he did to the last man who disobeyed him?"

"I know, I know." Crawford said in a placating tone. "It's just that they have so much they're sitting on up in that mountain, with no intention of sharing it with anyone. It's ours for the taking. I know the set up."

"Don't worry. McGee has a plan. He sent a rover over to Pueblo to get his brother, Lucky. I guess Lucky took over what's left of the city, but they're running out of food and most of the women have died. Once they get here, we'll have enough man power to overtake Manitou."

"I know how to get to the place and the basic layout of the area," Crawford preened. "I can't wait to see the surprise on Tanner's face right before I shoot him in the head." Crawford's mouth twisted into a slow smile.

The two men resumed their walk, heading back toward the campsite, their voices fading. When they were out of sight, Tanner took a deep breath that he hadn't realized he was holding. Crouching low and staying out of sight, Tweeny and Shelton were soon at his side.

"We got trouble," gasped Shelton.

"Looks that way," agreed Tweeny. "Did you hear enough?" He turned toward Tanner.

"I think their message was pretty loud and clear," Tanner growled. "I should have killed Crawford when I had the chance. Let's get back home."

Backtracking, they headed south beside the river. There had once been a park through here, the river on one side, and the interstate highway on the other. The peacefulness of the river trail was always in such sharp contrast to the noise of the freeway on the other side. The river had run right through the middle of the city and this small section had been set aside for the park.

After they had traveled over a mile and the camp was far enough away so they wouldn't be seen, they crossed back over the river, heading west. Nearly waist high, the river ran clear and smelled clean. The cold water was refreshing after the heat of another day. And the days were always hot.

When he was older, after the destruction, Tanner realized the river had a unique resonance all its own as it undulated and rippled with flowing life. He couldn't really describe the noise, maybe a soft swoosh. When young, he could never hear it above the noise of the traffic. Sure, it flowed but it didn't seem alive. Now the old highway was silent and the river was noisy, alive in its vigor.

How funny, Tanner thought, that nature had receded in the face of civilization's progress and now, with civilization's destruction, it had seemingly rebounded, as if it had never been gone to begin with. And he knew it hadn't.

Nature had only become the backdrop to human folly, inconsequential to human perception. Even he had been guilty of not truly seeing nature in the forefront until it was thrust upon him. What was it Thoreau had said? Something about erecting a ceiling between oneself and the sky only to realize the sky was still there so why bother. He would have to check that book out again.

Dripping cool water from the river, they carefully approached the old freeway. It was quiet. There seemed to be no one around. They crossed the shattered road on a strip of grass that had grown between two sections of pavement. Burnt out and rusted cars were still scattered about as if they had been dropped by a giant hand. The highway itself was destroyed, with only sections here and there remaining.

A rover could still follow a highway and know where he was going, but it would be impossible to drive on one, if there were cars to drive. In the beginning people had tried to get around in cars, but with no one to repair the roads or the cars and gasoline becoming scarce, it soon became impossible. It was easier to walk.

Fifteen years ago, in his roving to the south, Tweeny had made it as far as Albuquerque. It was destroyed, but people, mostly Navajo who had lived in the area, were trying to survive in a settlement by the Rio Grande River. That's where he met Shelton, a tribal member. Tweeny had wanted to continue on to Phoenix, but was told it was too dangerous.

Once out of New Mexico, gangs of bandits controlled the main thruways in Arizona or what was left of them. According to the Navajo, Phoenix had been destroyed at the beginning of the aftermath. Those who had survived had tried to trek northward, but there was nowhere to go and no one to welcome them. Most had perished on the journey.

Many of the bandits were former survivalists who had survived the hardships at the beginning and considered the roadways their territory and anyone traveling on them in their jurisdiction to be robbed, killed, or enslaved. When Tweeny heard this, he decided to return to Manitou. Shelton had expressed the desire to become a rover and, with his tribe's blessing, had left with Tweeny, becoming his apprentice of sorts.

66

Tanner gazed at Tweeny, lean, wiry and alert with Shelton by his side, quiet, stoic, long black hair in two braids. He trusted them with his life and knew they felt the same way. Having reached the foothills near the Garden, just as the sun was setting and the sky was darkening, Tanner decided to make camp.

Looking around at the towering sandstone rock formations, Tanner understood why it had once been a tourist attraction, a true geological wonder. It was nestled in an area where the grasslands of the plains met the pinion and juniper woodlands before merging with the mountain forest.

As Tanner understood it, before people had permanently settled here, two surveyors had come upon the beautiful area. One of them declared it was a fit place for the Gods to assemble, so he called it the Garden of the Gods. The name stuck. It had been shortened to the Garden since the aftermath. Many of the rock formations had fallen and were now strewn about the ground hap hazardously, as if Zeus himself had raged against the follies of man.

They could camp among the rocks, out of sight and fairly safe from marauders and night stalkers. Early tomorrow they would continue on and probably make it back by late morning. Sheltered by a rock overhang and giant slabs of sandstone on both sides, Tweeny started a small fire. They each carried a pack with supplies. Deciding against hunting for their dinner, they grabbed some jerky and crusty bread from their packs and got comfortable around the fire.

As they ate, they watched the sparks from the fire rise and disappear into the black night above them. They felt completely and utterly alone in the peaceful darkness, the only sound sizzling pops and whispering hisses of the fire.

Tanner said quietly, "You know, this changes everything."

Both Shelton and Tweeny glanced up. "How so?" Tweeny asked, breaking a twig and tossing it into the writhing flames.

"This whole area along the eastern Rocky Mountains from Pueblo to south of Denver has been relatively safe. We've been living peacefully and small colonies have even begun to thrive. Now, with McGee planning some sort of takeover, we are going to have to fight for our territory. We've never really had to battle anyone but the night stalkers and the occasional brigand."

"Sounds like he's getting help, too," Tweeny added. "Desperate men will do almost anything."

"Well, we are going to stop them," Tanner answered, frowning into the fire. "Tomorrow, we'll split up and you two go north to academy. You'll be safer going together. See Mitch; tell him what's happening. He may not be safe either. I'll head back home and warn the others. You two head back after you talk to Mitch." Tweeny and Shelton nodded their agreement.

As orange flames danced, casting flickering shadows on their faces, they slowly relaxed into the night. Soon the fire's dancing light began to fade, and Shelton stood up, taking the first watch. He disappeared into the night, the inky blackness enveloping him completely. Before Tanner drifted off to sleep, he glanced up at the star filled night and once again cursed humanity.

Chapter Eleven

Elizabeth juggled an armload of books as she walked over to the notebook on the small table at the entrance to the library. She set the books down on the shelf and recorded the books, officially checking them out. Overjoyed with the prospect of reading, she walked out of the library, waved at Sam and headed back to her new room. She was amazed and relieved at how much more comfortable she felt here than in the cabin.

Once in her room, she sat on the soft, cushioned chair, set her books on the small table, and for the first time since she woke up not knowing who she was, she relaxed. On the wall, facing the bed was a painting of a forest at night with the moon shining through the trees, illuminating the surroundings.

A peaceful feeling settled over her as she gazed at the picture. Dreamily, she saw the moon seem to fade away and the stars brightness pierced the darkness. The landscape grew darker as she slipped into a deep sleep.

Elizabeth awoke with a start. A sudden commotion outside had yanked her from her sleep. She glanced at the clock on the nightstand. It was ten in the evening. She had slept all afternoon and evening. Jumping up, she scrambled to the door, opened it and looked out into the hallway. James was outside her door running toward her. He saw her but didn't slow down.

"Everything is fine. I need to help Merlin."

"What? Is he okay?"

"Yes, he's fine." James yelled over his shoulder. "Just a small medical emergency. I'm sure he wants you to stay here."

Elizabeth started after him. If her behavior was any indication, she didn't think she was very good at doing what she was told. Finally arriving at the entrance, she saw James bending over someone on the gurney. The lights were much dimmer than before and a strange muted sound emanated from inside the room. She was afraid Merlin was injured.

Elizabeth stopped dead in her tracks. It was not Merlin on the gurney. Yellow, pain-filled eyes stared at her. Merlin pushed her aside as he came in from a side door holding a needle. The sound intensified and the night stalker grabbed his head. Blood was coming out of his ear. Merlin plunged the needle into his arm and he went limp.

"What are you doing here?" Merlin snapped, turning his head in her direction.

"I was worried about you. What is…?"

"Sit." Merlin motioned to the chair on the side of the room. He then grabbed a surgical knife and sliced into his patient's ear. Embedded an inch under his skin, above his eardrum was a small device. Using tweezers, Merlin pulled it out, the muted sound from the device becoming an ear-splitting peal. Elizabeth put her hands to her ears. Merlin laid the device in the sink, opened a cupboard and pulled out a large hammer. He slammed it down, creating an instant and welcoming silence.

"That takes care of that." Merlin stated emphatically.

"Can you tell me what's going on?" Elizabeth asked, confused, her gaze moving from Merlin to the strange and totally zonked-out patient and back again to Merlin.

Merlin held up his hand. "Hold on. James, clean the wound. I am going to stitch it up." While James was cleaning the area in and around the ear, Merlin grabbed his materials and walked back to his patient. Finished, James moved aside and Merlin began stitching the cut he had made.

"I was outside just as darkness fell," Merlin began. "All of a sudden, the wolves started howling like crazy." Merlin finished the last stitch and looked up at Elizabeth.

"I suspected night stalkers, so I started running back to the cabin because the fire had gone down. Before I reached it, he…" Merlin pointed at his patient. "He came out of the trees toward me. I pulled my gun out at the same time Raini

71

came out of the brush, her string in her bow drawn tight, her arrow aimed at his heart. He stopped, looked up in fear and pain and said two words."

Merlin took his supplies to the counter and washed his hands then leaned against the sink for a moment.

"What did he say?" Elizabeth quietly asked.

"He said 'help me'." Merlin walked back to the gurney, staring at the night stalker. "Two simple words and, beneath the yellow eyes and haggard bearing, I saw his humanity and I could not kill him. Then he collapsed, holding his head and that's when I heard the faint, high-pitched squeal. With Jom's help, I got him down here and you know the rest."

James was busy cleaning tools and equipment at the sink as Elizabeth and Merlin gazed at their unexpected patient. Elizabeth noticed his small, too slender frame and, with his eyes closed as if sleeping, an incongruous innocence radiated from his pale features.

He looked to be the age of Jom and Raini, dressed in ragged, dirty clothing, and on his feet were old shoes, with holes in the bottom. Any skin that showed seemed ingrained with dirt as if had become part of his skin. Elizabeth looked away, a quiet sob stuck in her throat. Merlin was more pragmatic.

"I am going to strap him down and post a guard until I can talk to him. This device in his head sheds a whole new light on the night stalkers. I'm pretty sure he didn't volunteer for the job. Someone was controlling him. That device is proof."

He pointed at the sink, his shrewd, bright eyes peering at her. "I believe you had a similar device in your arm. Someone took it out before you got here."

Chapter Twelve

Tanner was awakened by a squeeze to his shoulder. Opening his eyes, he saw Tweeny turn away and pick up a stick to prod the dying embers of the campfire. It was early morning with sunlight peeking over the eastern horizon, casting away the dawn hues of pink and yellow as it brightened the sky.

"Why didn't you wake me up three hours ago to take the last watch?"

Tweeny shrugged. "I wasn't tired."

Tanner didn't know what to say to that. He appreciated the favor. Getting up quickly, he stretched toward the welcoming rays of the sun. Shelton strode out

74

silently from behind a rock, chewing a strip of elk jerky. He handed one to Tanner.

"Thanks." Chewing on the jerky, Tanner gazed at Shelton and Tweeny. He knew the danger they were in. Rovers had an especially dangerous job, but these two were the best. He trusted them with his life.

"When you see Mitch, tell him what we know and see if you can find out anything else. Then, head back to Manitou and most important be careful. Don't take any chances by confronting anyone." Shelton and Tweeny nodded.

Tweeny poured water on the last of the embers. He and Shelton then turned to leave, heading north to Academy. Tanner rolled up his blanket, put it in his pack and headed west toward Manitou. If he hurried, he should get there by early afternoon.

Making his way out of the giant rocks of the garden and into forestland, his thoughts turned once again to before, before the aftermath. What a difference twenty years had made. The old highway they used to take from here was over grown and barely negligible. The grass and trees were reclaiming what was once theirs. The trip from the garden to Manitou was once a ten-minute trip by automobile, now it would take him all morning.

He quietly hummed an old tune. A twenty-year old tune he wryly thought, as he quickly hiked the slowly rising ground into the foothills of the mountains. His thoughts drifted as he walked. No new music had been created since the aftermath. The latest popular song was gone like everything else that had seemed an important part of society.

Once, he reminisced, there had been a proliferation of new music seemingly weekly and musicians churning out hits continuously to keep at the top of their game, knowing their success depended on their latest hit. Celebrities were being created out of nowhere, their celebrity based on false illusions. When that world had blown apart, the star making machinery had ground to a halt.

Looking back on it from a much quieter existence, it now seemed incredibly frivolous and silly. He didn't miss the gigantic, out of control social media that had dominated life back then. Nor did he miss the fast pace. Things had definitely slowed down. He had time to think now and to feel himself actually living, not going through the motions.

Still, he realized mankind had lost many of the beneficial aspects of society also. In the end so much of society's creations and inventions had been taken for granted that now even small things like a cell phone seemed like a luxury.

As he trudged along, he couldn't help but relish the idea of a faster mode of travel. He was used to walking, that was the reality of their world, but today he was impatient to get home and prepare to defend it.

Later that morning, Tanner stopped momentarily southeast of what was once the tourist town of Manitou Springs. The river had flooded the town so many times in the last twenty years there really wasn't much of a town left. Nature had reclaimed itself here also. Most of the buildings and roads were gone. Wild flowers bloomed along the well-worn path beside the river. North of town a few cabins still stood. An old friend lived in one of them but he didn't have time to visit today.

The path split and he headed south away from the river. He was now only a short distance from home. Tired and hot, Tanner once again found himself appreciating the comforts of his home. Merlin had created a utopia on a bleak world and he would protect it with his life.

Pondering what to do with his new arrival, he knew she would need the protection of the caves when the cabin was attacked. He really had no other choice but to let her inside. Without a doubt, Crawford would lead McGee's men right to the cabin door.

Once in the forest outside the cabin, he signaled the guards and they responded. He was flooded with relief to be home. Reaching the cabin door, he strode inside calling out for Merlin. The door to the bedroom was closed. She must be sleeping he thought and Merlin is probably inside the shelter.

He pushed the lever to the hidden door, stepping into the dim tunnel on the other side of the threshold and headed toward the medical facilities. He felt a sense of peace as he walked the familiar tunnel. As the tension left his body, he took a deep breath. Things were normal. Why shouldn't they be?

He entered Merlin's lab and came to an abrupt standstill, frozen in place. Normal was not what he would call the sight in front of him. Not only was their new arrival, Elizabeth, down here looking right at home. Directly in front of her lying on a bed in the unusually dim room was someone who looked very much like a night stalker. Had the world gone mad? Growling, he raised his rifle and aimed.

Chapter Thirteen

Elizabeth jumped when she heard a noise behind her. Seeing Tanner with his gun pointed directly at their patient, she could only gape. Merlin came out of his office, arms waving. "Tanner, put that away."

Tanner kept the rifle pointing at the night stalker. "What is going on here, Merlin? I leave for two days and when I arrive not only do I find her down here but down here with a night stalker."

"If you would lower your rifle, I will explain."

Realizing the night stalker was strapped at the wrists to the bed, Tanner grunted and slowly lowered his weapon. "This better be good, Merlin."

"I assure you, it will all make sense."

He walked Tanner out into the hall and quietly began his story, telling Tanner that Elizabeth was now staying in a dorm room because he trusted her and she felt more comfortable down here. As for the night stalker, he explained what happened the previous evening and showed him the destroyed device he had taken out of the night stalker's head.

Stunned, Tanner took it from him, turning it over in his hand. "This was somehow controlling him?"

"Yes, I believe so. He had just regained consciousness when you barged in. I was going to talk to him now."

Merlin walked back inside and sat in a chair beside his bed. Tanner remained in the doorway, arms folded across his chest.

Merlin began. "Hello, I'm Merlin. This is Elizabeth and Tanner." Elizabeth managed a slight smile. Tanner didn't even try.

Merlin glanced at Tanner then continued. "Do you have a name?"

The night stalker looked puzzled then his face brightened. "I have been called 47, but before I had another name. It was Laden."

"Before?"

"Yes, before I was captured by the…they call themselves the gods, our gods. Their power is great. They can talk inside our heads. All the lesser people must obey them. If they do not, the gods vent their disapproval and fury inside our heads. Many have died, when they have not obeyed."

He hesitated and shook his head. "They are no longer talking in my head."

Merlin studied Laden. "Before…where were you before you were captured?"

Laden frowned. "I lived in Pueblo in a new encampment with my mom. My dad died in the early days. I was gathering wood and it got dark before I made it back. I was captured by the yellow-eyes and they took me to the home of the gods."

Merlin gasped in disbelief. "You were not born with yellow eyes? You could go out during the day?"

"Yes, before I could, but no longer. It is too painful."

"Where is the home of these gods?" Tanner asked.

"On the other side of this mountain, to the south." He shuddered visibly. "I do not know how long I have been there. I was captured when I was ten."

"You look to be about sixteen or so," Merlin responded. "I would like to examine your eyes and see what was done to them. We thought people like you were mutants, your defective eyes caused by the radiation. Now it appears you were changed by some sort of procedure to your eyes and controlled by this device planted inside your ear." He held up the crushed device.

Laden stared in confusion. "I have disobeyed the gods, but they are not speaking to me or screaming in my head. Is that... that device somehow connected to them?"

"Exactly so." Merlin laid the device on the counter top by the sink. "They are no more gods than you or me. They simply controlled you with that device. You are now free of them."

Laden visibly relaxed. Then he stiffened again. "What if they come looking for me?"

Tanner stepped forward. "He has a point. If you destroyed that device here, they may now know our location. If they are controlling the night stalkers and sending them out to collect people into slavery, I don't think they are particularly pleasant people."

`Elizabeth remained silent, though visibly shaken. Her thoughts kept returning to Merlin's statement about her arm. Could she have been a part of that? She certainly hoped not. What kind of people hunted humans for slavery?

"Merlin, can I speak to you for a moment?" Tanner nodded toward the doorway to the tunnel. Merlin nodded and followed Tanner out into the tunnel away from the entrance.

"We have a problem." Tanner said. ""Crawford is with McGee and he is planning to lead him and his men back here. It's not for a friendly chat."

"I knew Crawford was trouble. I was hoping he would just disappear. How soon do you think it will take them?"

"Well, they're waiting for McGee's brother from Pueblo, so I would say we have one, maybe two weeks."

"We can withstand the onslaught," Merlin said confidently. "There is no way they can get through our defenses."

"Agreed. We will need everyone inside when we spot them approaching. I don't want to lose any of our people." Together they started back to the entrance, Merlin stopping to talk to a worker. Tanner went ahead.

"Have you ever seen me before?" Tanner heard Elizabeth quietly ask Laden as he entered the room. There was a moment's look of confusion on Laden's face as he studied her then he shook his head.

Noticing Tanner in the room, Laden looked toward the doorway and Elizabeth followed his gaze. When she saw him, Tanner briefly saw fear in her eyes before she looked away. Elizabeth noticed a faint hint of suspicion in Tanner's dark eyes, but to her great relief, he said nothing as Merlin entered behind him.

"Party's over," Merlin quipped. "My patient needs rest."

Elizabeth stood up quickly and left, heading to her room. She didn't want Tanner asking any questions she couldn't answer.

Tanner started to follow Elizabeth, curious about her question to Laden and wanting some answers. Merlin grabbed him by the arm, halting the younger man as he moved away.

"Merlin, I just want to ask her a couple of questions."

"They can wait. Come with me."

Merlin led him into his office and closed the door.

Exasperated, Tanner plopped down on the chair, putting his elbows on his knees and his head between his hands. He looked up at Merlin. "She asked him if he knew her. What kind of question is that?"

"A pretty smart one if you don't have any memory of who you are."

"How would he know her unless he knew her before his capture or they just recently came from the same place?" Sitting up straight, he stared at Merlin.

Merlin looked down and sighed.

"Merlin, what do you know?"

"I'm beginning to think maybe they did come from the same place."

"What?"

"Do you remember that deep cut on her forearm?"

Frowning, Tanner nodded.

"I believe she had some king of tracking device in her arm and it had been cut out before you found her."

Tanner stared at Merlin in disbelief. "This just keeps getting better and better. Where is this 'same place' you think they both came from?"

"I don't know, but with Laden's help, that's exactly what we're going to find out."

Chapter Fourteen

A tense week passed. Tweeny and Shelton had returned on the second day with nothing new to report. The academy settlement was on alert but could be of no help to them. They were on the defensive. McGee's men had been raiding their camp.

After resting a day, Tweeny and Shelton headed out toward Pueblo. They were watching the trail from Pueblo to observe any build-up of men heading toward McGee's camp. They had not returned yet.

Elizabeth found herself drawn to the gardens. She felt at peace when she was there and volunteered to help if they needed it. Marsha was grateful. She had her hands full with the animals and needed extra help in planting and harvesting their crops, drying herbs, and sorting and preparing seeds. Elizabeth had not seen Tanner during the past week. According to Merlin, he was busy preparing for the upcoming confrontation.

She had visited Laden every day. Being an outsider, she knew how he felt. He was now well enough to be in her dorm, just a few doors down from her. With clean clothes and a shower and some regular meals, he was beginning to look like a healthy teenager. His dirty blonde hair was more of a golden brown and the barber, James in his spare time, had trimmed it and it now waved naturally around his ears and neck.

There was still a guard posted outside his door, but he was free to go into the residential area and the dining area. Merlin had given Laden large tinted goggles that covered his eyes and were tight against his forehead on top and cheeks underneath. He was able to walk around without being bothered by the lighting.

Yesterday she was surprised when she heard Jom and Raini talking and laughing with Laden when she walked by his room. She popped her head in and waved. Jom told her he was impressed by the sunglasses and was going to ask Merlin to find a pair for him and Raini to wear outside. Elizabeth agreed they were a very fashionable accessory and left smiling.

Elizabeth was becoming more comfortable in her surroundings every day. The sunlight didn't bother her eyes as much. Unfortunately, she was still unable to remember anything of significance. Sighing, she approached the garden area, intent upon weeding the vegetable patch.

85

After gathering her tools and saying hello to Marsha, she found an area in need of weeding. She spent the morning bending and pulling at weeds. By lunchtime her muscles were aching and she could feel knots of tension in her neck and shoulders. Elizabeth rubbed the back of her neck, easing the tiny prickles that bit into her skin. It was time for a break.

She was on her way to the dining hall when she heard a commotion from the direction of the cabin. Merlin ran by, stopping briefly to tell her to stay in the dining area where it was safe. They would see that a guard was posted in the doorway. Merlin rushed toward the entrance to the cabin. Elizabeth hurried into the dining hall and over to the counter at the back where Gertie and her kitchen staff were huddled together, talking quietly.

"Do you know what's going on?" Elizabeth asked.

"Tweeny and Shelton just got back to the cabin," answered Gertie. "They told Tanner that McGee and his men are headed this way." Elizabeth could see the fear in her eyes. "I don't know much more than that."

"From all the preparation this week, I think things are under control out there." Elizabeth grabbed her hand and gently squeezed.

Gertie sighed. "I know. I'm just worried. We have so much to lose."

Elizabeth could understand her fear. Although she had only been here a little over a week, it was beginning to feel like home. Of course, she didn't have anything to compare it to. It just felt right.

"Well, let's get you something to eat. It is lunch time." Gertie stepped behind the counter. "Today, we have tomato soup and salad or an egg sandwich."

"I'll take the soup and sandwich. Thank you."

Elizabeth didn't realized how hungry she had become as she tried not to wolf down her food when it arrived. Gertie disappeared in the back, getting more food ready. Others had arrived to eat and there was a soft murmur of voices around her. Finishing up, she looked back at the entrance and noticed Merlin in the doorway. He hurried toward her and sat on the stool beside her at the counter.

"Have you heard the news?" he asked.

She nodded. "Are they here?"

Merlin shook his head. "The outside guards say they are camped about a mile away. We believe they will probably attack at nightfall."

"You have people outside still?"

Merlin didn't meet her gaze.

"No, please don't tell me Jom and Raini are outside. They are aren't they?"

Merlin was silent for a few moments and then sighed softly. "They would not come in if I asked. It's their job and they are very good at staying hidden. They remain in the treetops, undetected."

Elizabeth did not feel much relieved by the news. "They're so young."

Merlin nodded. "In years, yes." He reached over and touched her hand. "Don't worry. We have been preparing for something like this for a long time. We are more than…" She lost the rest of what he was saying as a loud explosion sounded from outside the cabin. Elizabeth's first instinct was to panic and run.

Merlin jumped up, "It's begun. They didn't wait for nightfall." He motioned for her to remain there and quickly headed back toward the cabin. When he stepped into the back entrance of the cabin, Tanner and his men were aiming their rifles through slits in the wall.

"What happened?"

"They threw some type of explosive at the cabin," Tanner yelled, firing a shot. "The wood is burning. They are going to be surprised when they realize the wood is just a front and it's going to be near impossible to get through the reinforced steel under it." He fired another shot and they heard a scream and a thump. A noise rocked the air again. The cabin shook.

Inside the dining hall, dirt fell from the ceiling onto the table. Elizabeth froze and looked up. What if it caves in? A seed of panic sprouted inside her, but she forced herself to stay composed. She saw fright in the eyes of those around her, but everyone managed to stay calm. Worried about Laden, she told Gertie she was going to check on him and she'd be right back. Gertie nodded at the guard and he let her pass.

Elizabeth headed toward the living quarters. It was much quieter away from the cabin. When she got to the hallway of the dorms, she noticed there was no guard by Laden's door, nor was there anyone at the back entrance. A knot of tension rose in her. She ran to his door and yanked it open. He wasn't there.

She hurried to the back entrance. Sam had returned and was sitting in his usual chair.

"Have you seen Laden?"

"No, why?"

"He's not in his room and the guard is gone."

"Oh, they needed Joe up at the cabin."

"Where were you a few minutes ago?"

"A man has to relieve himself now and again, missy."

Elizabeth felt a red flush creeping up her face.

"Oh, sorry. Of course." She turned to look for Laden when she noticed the back entrance door wasn't latched from the inside.

"Sam, did somebody go out that way?"

"Huh? No, why?" He looked at the door and bolted up. "That was locked up tight." He quickly secured it and looked at the monitor. "No one out there."

"Why would the door not be secured?"

Sam gestured toward the door, "Someone went out this way. It will still lock from the outside, but whoever leaves can't pull the inside latch across."

Suddenly Elizabeth knew. "Oh, no. Laden. He went out there. I just know he did. I have to find him." She headed for the entrance, terrified about going outside, but too worried to stay.

"Hold on. You can't go out there." Sam grabbed her arm. "There is a fight going on and no one can leave without permission from Tanner." He looked at her frightened face and gentled his voice. "Sorry, boss's rules."

Letting go of her arm, he added, "One of the guys probably had to leave in a hurry and couldn't wait for me to get back here. Laden is probably in the rec room or he went to get something to eat."

"You're probably right," Elizabeth sighed. "I'm over reacting. It's just... I just want to make sure he's safe."

"I understand," Joe replied. "Seems like a nice kid, once you get used to those eyes. Still, it's too dangerous out there right now. It's no place for a lady. Do you know what those thugs would do to a pretty woman like you?"

"Raini is out there. What about her?"

"Raini can take care of herself."

Chapter Fifteen

Raini pulled her bow up instinctively, aiming her arrow at the men below. Their approach happened so fast she, Jom, and Jesse didn't have time to get back to the cabin. Her arm trembled. She had never killed a man before. Unable to see clearly through the trees, she could still hear the shots being fired and loud explosions. The smell of burning wood was in the air.

Jom and Jesse were situated in nearby trees. Tanner said they should only defend themselves if they were stuck out here. A bullet whizzed by Jom. Someone had spotted him. He turned to conceal himself behind the wide part of the tree but was too late. Another bullet sliced into his shoulder, throwing him off balance. He toppled from his perch and hit two branches on his way down. They painfully slowed his descent but he still hit the ground with a loud thump.

With his breath knocked out of him, Jom lay momentarily dazed. Someone appeared above him and kicked him in the ribs. Jom groaned in pain as he tried to get up. Raising his rifle, his assailant smashed him in the head with the butt of it. Jom collapsed in a heap.

In horror, Raini watched the scene unfold below her. She tried to get a shot at the man over Jom but was unable to get a clear view as he was mostly hidden behind the tree. Raini couldn't see him as he headed toward the cabin. No one else was coming up the ridge. They were all converging around the cabin.

She quickly slipped down the tree and knelt at Jom's body. What she saw there made her heart pound in her chest. Jom was a mass of bruises and blood, his head battered and bleeding. Although unconscious, he was still breathing.

Trying to dampen the panic flaring in her, she assessed his wounds.

Before she could process the damage, an arm slipped around her neck from behind and she was yanked off her feet. She gripped her knife and desperately swung it backward. She missed and her assailant punched her wrist hard and the knife fell out of her hand. Feeling her breath being squeezed out of her as she was dragged away from her brother, Raini gagged, gasping for breath. Her lungs ached as her airway was cut off.

He loosened his hold and harshly whispered in her ear. "Don't try anything or you'll be dead." Gulping for air, she suddenly froze as recognition overwhelmed her, Crawford. She began struggling again and Crawford punched her in the side of the face, sending a burst of pain through her cheek.

Keeping her locked in his grip with his arm, he held a gun to her head with his other hand. She stopped struggling, realizing it was pointless. Terror and pain lit up her nerves as Crawford pulled her back into the woods farther away from the cabin.

"Leave her alone," Jesse stepped out from behind a tree, an arrow aimed at Crawford.

"Hey, I was just getting her out of danger." Crawford raised his hands and threw his gun to the ground. Raini stumbled away.

Distracted, Jesse glanced at Raini. Within that second, Crawford grabbed a gun tucked into the back of his belt. The deafening sound of gunfire split the air. Raini looked on in horror as Jesse collapsed to the ground, blood spreading across his shirt.

Terrified, Raini tried to scramble away from Crawford. Lunging toward her, Crawford easily grabbed her and pulled her deeper into the woods. Her last glimpse of Jesse was his broken body lying on the ground, his bow and arrow crushed under his arm.

Fear and anxiety slammed into her. Crawford dragged her around a giant boulder and threw her down, aiming his gun at her head.

"You want to end up like your friend?' Raini said nothing. "I didn't think so. After we have a little fun, we'll see what they'll give for you in exchange for your life. Your life for... well, what is your life worth, huh?"

Her heart racing, she slowly sat up, wanting to bolt, but knowing she wouldn't get very far. Crawford got out some rope and tied her hands behind her back. "Cooperate and I'll go easy on you," Crawford snickered.

He shoved her to the ground. His body was instantly on top of her, his weight nearly knocking the air from her lungs. She could smell his rancid breath. It was so repulsive, her stomach actually heaved. He was too heavy and she couldn't fight him and was horrified at the thought of what he would do. Raw fear erupted within her.

Rational thinking failed her. Crawford's eyes gleamed in victory as he ripped her shirt open, exposing her bra. Raini screamed in terror. His malicious laughter filled the air as he groped her body, when suddenly his eyes widened in shock and pain. He jolted backward, convulsing and howling in agony and fell heavily to the side of her. He

93

lay motionless, a knife sticking out of his back. Blood stained his shirt.

She jerked her head up and sobbed for joy when she realized it was Laden. He was frozen in place, eyes hidden behind the dark lenses of the goggles. A more strange and beautiful sight she had never seen. He pulled the knife, her knife, from Crawford's back and wiped it off on Crawford's shirt.

Gently wrapping his arms around her, he drew her up into a sitting position then cut the rope around her wrists. With trembling hands, she pulled her shirt together, tying the bottom of it as best she could."

"Are you alright? He didn't...?"

"No, no, I'm fine. If you hadn't got here when you did..." She looked around and whispered. "Crawford shot Jesse. I think he's dead."

Laden looked at her and nodded.

He handed Raini her knife. "Can you walk okay? We need to get back to Jom. We can't help Jesse but Jom was still alive when I came searching for you."

"Oh God! Jom!" Raini tried getting up only to stagger sideways, woozy from the hit on her head. Laden grabbed her arm to steady her.

"We've got to get back and help him," Raini murmured.

They heard voices filtering through the trees. "Quick behind that outcropping," Laden urgently whispered. He glanced at the body, but there was nothing they could do to hide it.

The voices abruptly stopped, their steps slowing down as they spotted Crawford's body. Raini and Laden crouched low, barely breathing.

"Whoa. What's this?" Momentary silence, then footsteps approached. "Looks like Crawford's dead."

"No loss there."

"If he wasn't already dead, I'd be tempted to kill him myself. Telling us how easy it would be to take over this place."

"Not so easy for him." Laughter. "I'm going back to Academy. McGee can fight his own battles."

"Yeah. I'm with you there. Let's get out of here." The voices faded as they moved down the ridge. Raini slowly let out the breath she didn't know she was holding.

"Let's stay hidden until we're sure it's clear," Laden whispered. "I think they've given up for now. It looks like McGee's going to lose some of his men."

"Hopefully all of them."

They leaned back against the rock, listening intently for the retreating men. More were noisily making their way through the trees and down the ridge. Soon it was quiet, all sounds of the fighting gone. Dusk began cloaking the landscape.

"I've got to get back to Jom," Rainy whispered in Laden's ear. Laden pointed to the backside of the outcropping. Raini nodded, and Laden helped her up. Keeping to the shadows, they quietly headed toward the cabin.

They spotted Jom's crumpled body under the tree. Raini knelt beside him, feeling for a pulse in his neck. It was very weak, but it was there. She breathed a sigh of relief. His breathing was shallow and his head wound still bled.

"We've got to get him back to the cabin before it's too late."

Chapter Sixteen

"What do you mean Laden's disappeared?" yelled Tanner. "And what are you doing here?"

Standing in the entrance to the cabin from the cave, Elizabeth almost cringed at Tanner's tone. Ignoring his last question, she answered, "I couldn't find him anywhere. I think he went out the back."

"Out the back?" Tanner roared.

This time Elizabeth did cringe. "You don't have to yell. My hearing is fine or it was. Hey, it's quiet out there."

"Yeah, they realized it was hopeless and left." Tanner looked over her shoulder. "Merlin what's going on?"

Merlin stepped around Elizabeth. "It seems the back entrance was unguarded momentarily and Laden slipped out that way."

"That's just great. We have a night stalker who knows all about us and is now doing God knows what with his yellow-eyed buddies. And now, thanks to you, he can even go out during the day."

"Maybe Jom or Raini spotted him," Merlin began. "Can we go outside yet?"

"We'll send the rovers out. Tweeny and Shelton check out the surrounding area and see if it's safe. See where McGee's men are heading and find Raini and Jom."

Tweeny and Shelton nodded and keeping their rifles in their hands walked toward the door. Tanner glanced out the slit once again to make sure all was clear.

"I don't believe it," he stared outside. "Hurry, open the door Tweeny. I'll be dammed."

When the door opened, Elizabeth saw Laden and Raini stumbling toward the cabin. Laden was carrying Jom on his back and helping an injured Raini.

Tanner rushed out of the cabin and Merlin ran to the cupboard, pulling out medical supplies. Near the cabin door, Laden stumbled backward but caught his balance as Tanner grabbed Jom and carried him into the room, placing him on the bed. Elizabeth hurried out to help Laden and Raini. Laden appeared unharmed, but Raini had a swelling on the side of her face and her clothes were torn and dirty.

"Are you alright?" Elizabeth put her arm around Raini and helped her through the doorway."

"I'm fine. It's Jom we have to worry about. He was shot and fell from the tree. Then one of McGee's men beat him up pretty badly. And Jesse…" Tears ran down her face.

"Jesse was shot," Laden said. "He's dead."

"What exactly happened out there?" Tanner asked quietly, his expression guarded.

'I ah… I went outside to help Jom and Raini," Laden stammered. "I found her knife and heard her scream and…"

"Crawford," Raini whispered. "Crawford was… he attacked me. I tried but I couldn't stop him." Her tear-filled eyes turned toward Tanner. "Crawford killed Jesse and Laden killed Crawford."

Tanner's eyes hardened. "I knew I should have killed that bastard when I had the chance." Softening his gaze, he went over to Raini and knelt beside her where she sat on the floor next to the foot of the bed, grasping her shoulders gently. "He didn't hurt you did he?"

Raini shook her head. "I'm a little bruised and battered, but no he didn't hurt me.
If Laden hadn't showed up when he did…" She involuntarily shivered. Tanner grabbed a folded blanket from the bed and wrapped it around her.

Attending to Jom, Merlin said, "He probably has a concussion. It looks like he got hit pretty hard on the head." Merlin then felt around his shoulder wound. "The bullet went through, so that's good. I'm more worried about his head wound."

Merlin cleaned up Jom's wounds and put bandages on them. He was pale and unconscious and Merlin knew it wasn't good. Elizabeth worried over Raini who insisted she was fine. Laden was sitting at the table not saying anything and Tanner stood at the front of the cabin, arms crossed, his expression inscrutable.

"We've got to get Jom to the medical facilities," Merlin fretted. "Laden will you get James and tell him to bring a stretcher."

Laden nodded and jumped up, eager to be of help.

Tanner grabbed his shoulder, halting him. "Thank you. I hate to say it but I owe you." Laden grinned and headed toward the entrance to the cave.

"We heard McGee's men talking as they retreated," Raini began, wiping at her tears. "Crawford is the one who got them interested in attacking us. He said it would be easy pickings. They talked about deserting McGee and heading back to Academy."

"That's good news. I will have Tweeny and Shelton follow them to make sure. Now, I need to help the men round up the bodies." He sighed, thinking of Jesse. "It's getting dark out there. We will bury them in the morning." Tanner walked out the front door.

Laden reappeared with James and they got Jom on the stretcher and were gone, with Merlin trailing them. Over his shoulder, he told Raini he wanted to check her face. Elizabeth helped Raini up and they followed them into the caves.

After getting Jom comfortable, Merlin looked over Raini's wounds. Her cheek was already beginning to swell and turn purple. He put some healing cream on it and told her it would look pretty bad for a couple of days.

With a comforting pat, he recommended she get some rest. She didn't want to be too far from Jom, so she went into another room close by and lay down. Merlin disappeared into his office.

Elizabeth sat beside Laden at Jom's bedside. "That was a very brave thing you did out there today."

He was silent for a moment and then sighed softly. "They would have done the same for me. It is the first time I have truly had friends since my capture. I wish I had gotten there sooner to help Jesse." Elizabeth smiled sadly.

Looking down at his hands, he went on. "I understand the value of friendship. We were kept isolated in Cheyenne Mountain. We were so alone. Friendships were forbidden, so mostly everyone kept to themselves or risk the wrath of the gods."

"How awful that must have been for you."

"Yes, I hated the gods who seemed so powerful." Laden took a deep breath, the resentment in his eyes fading, leaving a lingering unhappiness. "I know now that they aren't gods at all but cruel men who will do anything for power."

"Yes," came a voice from the door. "And we need your help to find these men and destroy their ability to enslave and control people. Will you help us Laden?" Tanner strode into the room.

Laden smiled slightly. "Of course, I will help you. You have given me my freedom and your friendship. That is treasured above all. Residuum needs to be stopped."

Something broke inside Elizabeth's mind. "What did you say?"

Laden looked puzzled. "I said yes. I will help."

"No," Elizabeth felt panic. "The name, what was the name?"

"The gods call themselves Residuum. Every day we were told, 'When all has been lost, Residuum is what remains. It is your life. It is your way to the truth.' That was our mantra."

"Are you okay?" Tanner asked. All the blood had drained from her face.

"Yes. No. That name. I know I have heard it before. I was suddenly overwhelmed by Laden's reference to it. That name, Residuum, it's familiar to me." Elizabeth frowned in concentration, her expression pinched. "Now, it's gone. I've drawn a blank again."

Hesitating a moment, Elizabeth looked from Laden to Tanner. "I want to come with you on your mission to the mountain," she blurted out.

"No." Tanner answered without hesitation. "It's too dangerous."

"But it might help me get my memory back. I can't live like this." Elizabeth put her head in her hands wanting to weep in frustration, but knowing she didn't want to appear weak in front of Tanner.

Tanner scooted a chair in front of Elizabeth and gently took her hands. "I am sorry. I can't risk your life on something this dangerous. You are still healing from your ordeal. You don't even like going outside."

Elizabeth realized the truth in that statement. "I know, it's just that… I need to know who I am and where I come from, no matter how unpleasant that truth may be."

"Give it time. You are beginning to remember in bits and pieces. It is just a matter of time." He squeezed her hands.

"Your right." Elizabeth paused. "It's just frightening to think I was part of this organization Laden speaks of."

"If you were, there is a good chance you were as manipulated as Laden, just in a different way."

"What do you mean?"

Tanner laughed. "Well for one thing, you don't have yellow eyes. Also, you seem to have lived a healthy, protected life even if you were kept in some sort of isolation.

102

Maybe it was an imprisonment you didn't realize you were in and that made it acceptable."

"Maybe something happened to change that," Elizabeth pondered. "Perhaps that's why I left."

Tanner released her hands and stood. "That is very possible. I believe one day…"

"Oh, my head," Jom's pained voice moaned from the bed.

Tanner turned and carefully sat on the side of the bed beside Jom. "Well, it looks like you're going to make it after all, not that I had any doubts. You're too stubborn to die."

"What happened? Last I remember I was in the tree taking shots at the enemy."

"You were doing a good job of it too, until you fell out of the tree."

Jom jolted upright, wincing at the pain in his head. "Raini. Where's Raini?"

"Hold on there," Tanner gently pushed him back into his pillow. "Raini is fine. She is getting some much-needed rest. Something you need, also. We'll tell you everything later."

Jom nodded, his eyes closing and falling almost immediately to sleep.

"Was that Jom I heard?" Merlin asked, hurrying out of his office. Tanner nodded.

Merlin glanced at the sleeping figure. "His color is much better."

He checked Jom's pulse and temperature. Satisfied, he nodded. "Jom just needs a good deal of rest, and he'll be up in the trees again before you know it." Merlin turned to go back to his office.

"Merlin, tomorrow night we are going in search of the mountain Laden says he came from. We need your help."

Chapter Seventeen

Merlin slowly turned back toward Tanner. "You know I'll help in any way I can. Tomorrow seems somewhat soon, though, doesn't it?"

"Not really," Tanner replied. "McGee and his men have dispersed, from what I gathered from Tweeny's report.

Most of the men are heading back to Academy and Mitch will keep them in line. McGee disappeared into the woods. He's probably heading to Pueblo to see if he can get help from his brother. I don't think Lucky will risk what he has to join his brother."

"You're right," Merlin said. "I will get my things ready and be prepared to go tomorrow evening."

"Merlin, I need your help, but I want you to stay here. Someone has to take charge if anything happens to me."

Merlin hesitated, contemplating Tanner's words. "Yes, I can understand that. What help do you need then?"

"I need a shot to knock someone out so they are unconscious for a while."

Puzzled, Merlin raised his brows, "Oh?"

"I figure we may see more night stalkers. If we can get another one, we can gain even more information, not to mention free them from their enslavement, now that we know they are not volunteering to be night stalkers."

Elizabeth could have hugged Tanner. Maybe he was more caring then she had first assumed upon meeting him.

"If he is unconscious," continued Tanner, "he won't have to go through the pain of the device screaming in his head like Laden did."

"Very unpleasant," Laden acknowledged.

"Makes sense," Merlin agreed. "Once you're back, I can remove it before he gains consciousness."

"From what Laden remembers, the mountain entrance is only a couple of hours from here. Hopefully, we can easily get back before he does gain consciousness."

Merlin nodded. "I am going to do some more work, and spend the night here in case Jom needs something in the middle of the night. I'll have what you need before you leave. See you tomorrow." Merlin retreated to his office.

"I'm going to my room and get some sleep," Laden got up and left.

Feeling awkward Elizabeth stood up to go. "Well, it's been a stressful day. I will see you tomorrow."

"Goodnight Elizabeth."

The following evening, Tanner, Laden, and Tweeny stood outside the cabin, ready to depart. They each had a small pack with water and food. Earlier in the day, Tweeny had given Laden some shooting lessons, and was surprised at his precision in hitting the target.

All of them were now armed with guns, knifes, and extra ammunition. Tanner carried a syringe in a protected case. The slanting rays of the sun cast orange hues across the sky. It would soon be dark. Laden had on his goggles until total darkness covered the land.

"Everyone ready?" Tanner asked. Tweeny and Laden nodded. He glanced over at Merlin and Elizabeth who were standing at the entrance to the cabin. It was the first time she had ventured outside.

Laden pointed at his head, "I no longer have the map in my head, but I think I can remember the way."

"A map?" Tanner inquired.

"Yes. Our controllers wanted to make sure we always found our way back. The correct route home was always there in my mind."

106

"The chip in your head. That is how they talked to you and controlled you. They also always knew where you were," Merlin explained. "They programmed a map into the chip and you were always able to see it and find your way. It will be harder now."

"I know, but remnants of the route home are still etched in my brain. I believe I can locate the entrance to Residuum."

"I'm betting on that," Tanner quipped. "Let's go. Laden, after you."

Elizabeth watched the trio disappear into the surrounding woods and approaching darkness. She sighed, apprehension and worry etched on her features. Merlin grabbed her hand and gently squeezed.

"It's alright. Don't fret. They are going to be fine and we will know more about your possible home when they return."

"I hope so. It is just so dangerous and I can't help but worry."

"Let's go inside and have some tea. I've got just the blend to help you relax." Elizabeth nodded and with one last glance at the darkening woods, followed Merlin inside.

Merlin bustled around the kitchen as Elizabeth sat at the table trying not to think about the danger Tanner, Tweeny, and Laden were in. Her thoughts turned to Residuum. What exactly are they up against and how was she a part of that? How could people change and enslave children to impose their will on them? She instinctively knew that was unethical and just plain wrong. Her worse fear was that she was somehow a part of that. She mused to herself with an inward grimace.

Noticing her frown, Merlin quietly reassured her, "Everything will be fine. We have to believe that."

Elizabeth smiled softly, "I know." She swirled the tea bag in the cup Merlin had set in front of her. "It's just that somehow I'm linked to Residuum and it's hard to reconcile myself to that fact. From what Laden has told us about them, they are a corrupt and controlling organization. I can't bear the thought of being part of that."

"Like Tanner said, you may have been as unaware and manipulated as Laden."

"Yes, logically, I understand that, but emotionally, my heart aches."

"It's a tough world we live in. Things are much different from before," Merlin sadly shook his head.

"Merlin, tell me what happened. What exactly caused the devastation and the end of the world as you knew it?"

Merlin sighed. "The lunar fiasco started it all."

"The lunar fiasco?"

"Yes. It all started when astronomers discovered a large meteor approaching earth. It was reported to be miles wide and it was headed directly at us. We only had a matter of months after it was spotted. Then came the realization that it would bypass the earth; however, it was on a direct trajectory toward our moon."

"Oh, my God," Elizabeth cried. "What happened?"

"Cheyenne Mountain, the government facility my wife worked at was developing a special wave function. They

108

believed this wave could prevent the meteor from striking earth."

"You are talking about the TAG wave, aren't you?"

"Yes, how did you know that?"

"I seem to have an enormous amount of knowledge about astrophysics." Elizabeth shrugged. "I wish that knowledge would transfer over to my personal memories."

Merlin studied her. "Many amnesia victims have experienced the same thing you have. Don't give up hope. I firmly believe your memories will return my dear."

"Thank you, Merlin."

Nodding, Merlin continued, "The TAG wave, or as you know Tesla's anti-gravity wave was the answer. Scientists believed they could create an anti-gravity field between the earth and the moon creating a void with no gravity, and the moon would fall toward earth, enough to get out of the direct path of the meteor. Once that was accomplished, the wave function would be shut down, restoring gravity and stabilizing the moon. The meteor would whiz by, avoiding impact, and continue on its journey through space. A few hundred miles was all that was needed, just enough to avoid the meteor."

"Yes, I understand the underlying principles."

"It sounded so straight forward. Vivien really thought it would work."

"Your wife?"

"Yes. She was working on the TAG wave project to the end. She never made it out of Cheyenne Mountain."

"I'm so sorry, Merlin."

"It really should have worked. It just took longer than they thought to generate the wave field. When the field reached its full potential, it was too late," Merlin sighed.

"The meteor hit the moon. It was a direct hit and with the wave function still on and no gravity to hold the moon in place, it was knocked out of the solar system. Before it disappeared, huge chunks of debris from the moon and the meteor hit the earth. China took the main brunt, with Tokyo taking a direct hit. It destroyed the city.

"Oh my god!" Elizabeth gasped.

The Chinese blamed the United States and said it was a planned attack on their country and they retaliated with missiles to our major cities. Our allies got involved and soon the whole world was deploying missiles and bombing one another. Colorado Springs was hit hard and Cheyenne Mountain was destroyed."

Elizabeth felt Merlin's despair. "How awful for you."

"She was going to leave as soon as they succeeded. I never dreamed it would turn out like it did. Soon after the failure, with chaos erupting worldwide, friends and family who could get here begin to show up and we withdrew into the caves. You know the rest from reading my journal."

Elizabeth nodded, not knowing what to say. Words seemed insufficient.

"Unfortunately, the result of the TAG wave experiment is not over. Without the moon to stabilize our orbit, we have gradually lost our axial tilt. The earth no longer has seasons. The poles are melting and the earth is slowly being flooded. We may not be high enough to avoid the water. That is what we fear now."

With dread creeping up her spine at Merlin's words, Elizabeth could only sit in stunned silence.

Chapter Eighteen

"I can't see a damned thing in front of my face," Tanner grumbled, stumbling again as he followed a fleet-footed Laden. "Without the moon, my night vision is really pathetic."

"Ah, but look at that night sky," Tweeny stopped and looked up in awe.

Tanner knew he was right. Although the earth had been cast in darkness when the moon was lost, the night sky was absolutely breath taking. He stopped alongside Tweeny and stared at the heavens. Bathed in a richness only a dark sky can create, they stood under a canopy of shimmering stars with the Milky Way sweeping a path across the heavens. The sparkling and dazzling night sky left Tanner and Tweeny momentarily transfixed as they peered upward.

Laden leaned against a tree and looked at them in amusement. "You two don't get out much at night do you?"

"No. You see, until recently, we have been trying to avoid night stalkers, not joining up with them and carousing around the countryside at night," Tanner returned. Tweeny chuckled quietly as they shuffled along through the darkness behind Laden.

Due to the operation on his eyes, Laden could see very well at night. They had brought flashlights but turned them off when he felt they were drawing near their destination. Having traveled about two hours, Laden was sure they were close to the mountain entrance. The trail seemed familiar to him.

"We are getting close," he murmured. Suddenly he came to a standstill, Tanner almost running into him.

"Please warn us when you plan to stop abruptly."

"Oh, sorry," Laden glanced around. "This is it." A dark shadow loomed in front of them.

"Not much of an entrance here," commented Tweeny.

"It opens up."

"Oh. I don't suppose you know how to open it."

"No, that wasn't on my list of night stalker duties."

Ignoring their banter, Tanner said, "We'll lay low for a while and see what happens. We're on the south side of Cheyenne Mountain. The main entrance is to the northeast of here about five miles around the mountain."

"Do you think this might be another entrance into the mountain? One nobody knew about," Tweeny asked.

"Possibly. If so, then the facility inside the mountain is still operational, but what they are now doing is anyone's guess."

"Considering what Laden has told us," Tweeny responded, "what they're doing is not good."

Tanner nodded, sitting down against a large boulder. "If the facility has become this Residuum Laden's been talking about and they are enslaving people, then yes there is a big problem here."

Laden began methodically searching the side of the mountain where he was certain the entrance was located. Tweeny sat across from Tanner with his back against a large pine tree. They could barely see Laden in the darkness.

An hour later and they were still waiting. Laden had given up and was sitting cross-legged on the ground beside Tanner and Tweeny. Without warning, a grating mechanical sound came from the side of the mountain Laden had been investigating. Everyone jumped up and rushed to the spot of the noise. A section of the mountain began to slide away, rocks and ground with it. It was a cover up for the entrance, which was wide enough to walk through.

Laden whispered in warning, "We need to hide. The night stalkers will be returning and they have very good eye sight." He pointed to a nearby rock outcropping and they hurried to it and got out of sight just in time

They heard the quiet approach of feet. There was no talking, just the hurried pace of feet over the ground and the sound of something being dragged. Without hesitation, the night stalkers stepped through the entrance disappearing into the darkness. Laden jumped up as the door begin to close and jammed a rock into the doorway. The door jerked once against the rock then stopped slightly ajar. There were no alarms of security breached, just an eerie silence. The mountain seemed to swallow the night stalkers.

"Laden, you and I are going in," Tanner said quietly. "Tweeny, wait out here."

Laden and Tweeny nodded. Keeping the rock in place, Tanner opened the door enough for them to squeeze through. They spent the next few minutes slowly making their way through a dark tunnel. Dim lights overhead were barely enough to see by.

"Up ahead is where I lived," Laden whispered.

Even with the warning, Tanner was shocked when they rounded the shadowy bend. Small cells had been carved into the side of the cave, each holding a cot. In the cots were the night stalkers, about thirty of them. They were lying there apparently sound asleep.

An area in front of the sleeping rooms held a couple of tables and some chairs. What looked like a large laundry chute was at the far end. Beside it, a red line ran across the floor, separating the living area from what was beyond: a tunnel that seemed to wind downward into the inky bowels of the mountain.

"I have never been beyond the red line," whispered Laden. "It is forbidden."

"Can we get by them?" Tanner whispered in Laden's ear.

"They put us to sleep for hours when we come back." He nodded toward the cots. "They will not awaken."

They slipped along as quietly as possible, traversing the room and reaching the red line. Pointing at the laundry chute, Laden whispered, "That's where we put anyone we capture. They disappear down the chute and then...I don't know. Some become night stalkers and the others..." he shrugged. Tanner slowly nodded.

He glanced up at a sign above the corridor, the words old and faded. Squinting in the darkness, with difficulty he read Cheyenne Mountain Military Installation. Merlin was right, he thought. It wasn't destroyed but what had it become? Apprehension touched him like cold fingers.

Taking a moment to get his bearings, Tanner felt his way along the tunnel using his hand, Laden beside him. As they progressed, the tunnel darkened even more, curving as it descended into blackness. After a few minutes, they saw a faint light ahead of them. A flight of stairs descended to a doorway with light shining through the top of the door.

Laden hesitated then grabbed his goggles out of his pocket and put them on. Pushing through the door, they found themselves in a well-lit corridor. A line of lights along the ceiling illuminated the passageway. At the end of the corridor was another door. As they drew near, they heard voices. Tanner shot Laden a glance and pointed to a small window at the top of the door.

Carefully stepping forward, they pressed against the door. Tanner, craning his neck to peek inside the window, saw two men sitting at a small table, playing cards.

A body lay sprawled at the bottom of the chute.

"Looks like those mindless idiots finally earned their keep last night," one of the men commented, glancing at the body.

"Yeah, Winston will be happy when we bring this one up to him," the other one laughed. "She'll go right to the breeding lab."

"I don't know. She looks kind of old for that."

"You know how the outside ages women. I'd say she's under thirty." He lifted her matted yellow hair covering her face and studied her. "Yeah, she'll do."

"Winston said they are up to five babies at a time per pregnancy. Working wombs, that's what he calls them," he laughed.

"Well, let's get her onto the back of the jeep and I'll drive her upstairs so they can decontaminate her, clean her up and prep her."

"I don't think so."

Both men jumped up at the voice from the doorway, their hands going for the guns at their side.

"Not a good idea. Raise your hands real slow like." Tanner growled, his rifle pointing at the two men. They did as he said, glaring at Tanner and Laden. Tanner nodded at the woman and Laden quickly walked over to her and picked her up.

"Hey that's our property," yelled one of the men. "How did you get in here? Who are you?"

Ignoring the questions, Tanner said, "She belongs to us. You stole her and we're getting her back. Turn around and keep your hands in the air. It's time for a nap." He grabbed the syringe out of his pack, walked over to the men and plunged it into the raised arm of one of the men, letting out half the serum. He withdrew it and plunged it into the other man's arm. Almost immediately, they fell heavily to the floor.

"Wow. That's strong stuff. That should keep them asleep for a couple of hours, enough time to investigate a little more.'

Tanner pointed to the unconscious woman. "We'll pick her up on the way back. Let's see what's up that corridor." He stepped toward it, Laden following, gripping his weapon tightly.

Just as they slipped past the jeep and rounded a corner, an alarm went off. "Intruder alert, intruder alert" the overhead speakers bellowed. Tanner and Laden burst into motion. Running back past the jeep, they stormed past the unconscious men, Tanner hurriedly picking up the woman and flinging her over his shoulder.

They barreled out the door and ran up the steps into the darkened tunnel. Darkness swallowed them as they stumbled through the corridor at a reckless speed. The dim light from the night stalkers' quarters came into view. Tanner was relieved until he saw dark shapes filling the entrance. The night stalkers were awake.

Tanner skidded to a halt, Laden nearly running into him. "Get out your flash light," Tanner yelled.

Already pulling it out of his pocket, Laden clicked on the flashlight and a beam of light danced through the air. As they moved rapidly ahead, the beam reached the entrance and a shrill cry rendered the air, the night stalkers effectively blinded by the light.

Taking advantage of that, Tanner and Laden plowed through the bodies. One night stalker let out a shrill cry as Tanner punched him in the stomach. Crossing the red line, Laden elbowed another one, plunging him down the chute.

The night stalkers continued thrashing out at them with eyes closed. Tanner bumped against them and one grabbed his leg. He kicked himself lose and finally got himself out of their reach. Laden was tackled from behind and went sprawling. He managed to get up on his hands and knees when someone jumped on him and started squeezing his neck. Gasping for breath, he twisted, trying to throw the attacker off. Tanner grabbed the night stalker and pulled him off, throwing him against the wall.

He picked up the woman as Laden scrambled to his feet. The bodies thinned. Many had retreated to the dim light, their pain filled eyes showing their inner torment. Tanner had no time to feel sympathy for their mental anguish.

Charging through the remaining men still flailing and clawing at them, Tanner and Laden somehow reached the other side. They hurried down the dimly lit corridor leading to the entrance into the mountain, Laden's flashlight pointing backward as a safeguard. Rounding a bend, they heard cries and footsteps in the distance as their pursuers gained their eyesight and courage in the dim light. The lights sputtered overhead.

With relief, they spotted the door to the outside and safety. Drawing near, with the cries behind them growing louder, they skidded to a stop, staring in disbelief. The door was completely closed; the rock holding it open gone.

Chapter Nineteen

Elizabeth could not sleep. Merlin's words kept resonating inside her head. Her view of the world was considerably diminished with her head injury and subsequent amnesia. She found it odd that she recollected all her knowledge of astronomy and science, yet nothing of her personal life. Her mind felt like a half completed jigsaw puzzle with the missing pieces just out of reach. Without the context of who she was, all her knowledge was just disassociated facts with no relevance.

Heaving a sigh of frustration and giving up on any thought of sleep, Elizabeth got out of bed. Stretching her arms over her head, she groggily turned back around to make the bed. Her hand accidentally hit a glass of water on the nightstand, sending it flying. Almost full, water spilled on the stand and onto the floor.

"How clumsy," she muttered, looking around for a towel to clean up the mess. Finding nothing, she slipped into the hall and found some hand towels on one of the bathroom shelves. Grabbing a couple, she went back to her room, the corridor quiet so early in the morning.

Stepping into her room, she hurried over to the nightstand. The small rug by her bed, wet underneath from the water spill, slipped out from under her feet. Losing her balance, she fell and landed on her back, her head hitting hard on the floor. An eerie numbness enveloped her mind, as she lay stunned, unable to move. Then everything went black.

*   *   *

Drip… Drip… That leaky faucet is making my head hurt, Elizabeth thought in a sleepy haze. She would have to fix it again. Maybe Pop could help her. He was so busy, but he always seemed to find time…time, we're almost out of time. Half formed thoughts engulfed her as she lay in a murky state between sleeping and awakening; it seemed important to hold onto them. Too ephemeral, they drifted away into a fog. She fell back into a heavy sleep.

Hours later, her eyes fluttered open. Disoriented, she looked around the room. Where was she? Her bewildered gaze fell upon the picture of the moon shining down on a darkened landscape. The image combined with the familiar dripping created a catalyst in her mind and without warning, two disparate worlds collided in her psyche. A sharp pain split her skull, lancing deep into her brain. She gripped her aching head in confusion as the past rushed in. Jumbled images, voices, and scenes played out in her mind, with the present bubbling up beside it.

"I remember," she moaned to herself. "I remember it all." She looked around the room as if seeing it for the first time. Water dripped off the nightstand onto the floor.

122

Groaning from the combined throbbing in her head and the mental distress in her mind, Elizabeth shakily sat up.

"Oh dear God," she cried out, reeling from the pain and the flood of memories. "What have I done? I have to go back." Sobbing in despair, she slid back onto the floor.

Chapter Twenty

"Ah, hell." Tanner deposited the unconscious woman on the ground and pushed on the door, trying to force it open. He couldn't see a latch or anything to pull on. He pounded on it, yelling for Tweeny. Behind them were the shrill cries of the night stalkers as they drew nearer.

Laden stepped in front of Tanner and the woman, flashlight in one hand, rifle in the other, peering nervously down the corridor. The light from his flashlight bounced off the sides of the walls sending shadows dancing down the tunnel into the gloom.

Within a heartbeat, everything changed. The sounds of the night stalkers ceased as if they were no longer in pursuit. Tanner threw a questioning look at Laden who shrugged uneasily. Just as quickly, the silence was replaced by a faint rumbling sound. As it got louder, Tanner recognized the sound as a vehicle moved toward them down the corridor.

"This is not good," Tanner muttered as he desperately felt along the sides of the door.

"We've got company," Laden called out in a harsh whisper. A jeep stopped about thirty yards away, bright headlights shining directly at them. Three men were perched on it, each with a rifle pointing at them.

The apparent leader yelled out, "Drop your weapons. You are unauthorized trespassers here." The lights overhead sputtered out

At that moment a shrill scream like a war cry erupted from behind the jeep. Two night stalkers, eyes crazed, leaped onto the back of the jeep. Taking advantage of the distraction, Laden shot the head lights out of the jeep and turned off his flashlight. The corridor was plunged into darkness.

Curses and shouts echoed through the narrow space of the corridor. Gunshots rang out. An agonizing scream filled the air. A bullet whizzed by Tanner's head and lodged in the wall. Pulse pounding in his neck, and sweat beading at his nape, he frantically felt along the inside for any kind of lever or handle to open the door. Nothing. Suddenly, a grating noise filled the cramped space. The door slowly swung open. Tanner stared in disbelief. In the dim light of early morning, he saw Tweeny standing to the side of the open door, a device in his hand, a crumpled body at his feet. Grinning, he waved at Tanner.

A scuffling sound was heard from the corridor as more shots were fired. Tanner grabbed the woman and quickly slipped out the door. Laden sprinted toward the opening, a barrage of bullets blasting the walls around him. Once Laden was safely outside, Tweeny pressed a button on the device and the door started to close. Tanner glanced back. Near the opening lay the dead body of a night stalker, bloody arm extended toward the entrance. The door banged shut.

The air shimmered with sunlight as Tanner struggled to keep his eyes open after the darkness inside the mountain. Brilliant, early morning light streamed over the ridge, casting away the gray hues of dawn as it brightened the sky.

"Let's get out of here," Tanner yelled, swiping at the tears starting in his eyes from the bright light. Laden pointed to the west. An obscure path wound its way into the woods. He ran toward it.

"I see you picked up someone on your way out," Tweeny muttered, pocketing the device and hurrying after Laden. Tanner followed closely behind, not bothering to answer. There was no sound of the door opening as they headed out. The shadows of the forest eased the painful glare of the sunlight.

After about an hour, they slowed down. There was still no sign of pursuit. Tanner, exhausted from the extra weight of the woman, stumbled. Tweeny suggested they rest briefly and then he would carry her. Nodding in agreement,

125

Tanner carefully laid the woman down and sank to the ground.

"What happened while we were in there?" Tanner asked, taking a big gulp of water and wiping his mouth with the back of his hand.

"Everything was fine until a guard seemed to come out of nowhere. I was hidden, but he noticed the rock holding the door open. He went to move it when I jumped him. He sounded the alarm on this device here." He pulled it out of his pocket and held it up. "Pretty handy device." He threw it to Tanner.

"In the scuffle, he kicked the rock out from the door." Tweeny went on. "I finally knocked him out with a rock. Right away I began examining that device, thinking maybe it was some kind of remote control." Tanner threw it back.

"Did you hear me yelling from inside?" Tanner asked.

"No. It's pretty sound proof in there. Imagine my surprise when the door opened and there you were."

"Quite the surprise for us, too. Your ugly face never looked so good," Tanner grinned.

"Thanks Tweeny," Laden said. "We were really in a jam."

"I kind of gathered that."

"Yeah, thanks, buddy," Tanner added. "You saved our lives back there." He stood up slowly, stretching his back. "And considering we may not be in the clear yet, we probably should get moving."

They started making their way through the forest again. Laden lead the way, maintaining a brisk pace. Tanner

126

gave Tweeny a rundown on the events that occurred inside the mountain and why they were now carrying an unknown woman with them. He relayed the conversation of the guards he and Laden had overheard and the sign he had read in the corridor.

"So it really is Cheyenne Mountain," Tweeny whistled under his breath. "It used to be a military facility. What happened?

"I don't know," Tanner shook his head. "We're not safe as long as they are stealing people and enslaving them. Something has gone terribly wrong inside that mountain."

Chapter Twenty One

Deep in the subterranean depths of Cheyenne Mountain, the acting president of Residuum, Winston Shell, thoughtfully studied the three men standing uncomfortably in front of his desk. His calm exterior hid the inner volcanic perturbations seething in his mind, threatening to spill out into the room. Only a well-honed internal self-control kept them at bay

Only twenty-eight, he had been groomed for this job for twenty years. His father, the first president, having taken command after the holocaust, had purposely created a hierarchical framework of presidential succession. Being the first son, when his father died five years ago, the job had automatically gone to him. His younger brother, Terrence, was naturally second in command. The succession had gone smoothly enough; no one had come forward to object.

Since establishing his authority, his plan had been progressing steadily until today. "So, the intruders were not apprehended," he stated flatly. "Tell me this, how did they manage to get inside our facility?"

Stuart, the one in charge, shook his head. "We're not sure. Larry told me that before one of the intruders drugged him, he said they were there to get the woman back. We think they might have followed the night stalkers to the entrance."

"This is unprecedented. No one follows the night stalkers. We have instilled fear in everyone on the outside. They run from night stalkers." Momentarily pondering the incident, he wondered if it had anything to do with 47 who went missing awhile back. He didn't believe in coincidences. And now, he had lost two more.

"We have never had a breech in our security. Ever. No one has ever gotten inside this facility." He leaned forward, hard gray eyes boring into the guards. "Why were they not apprehended?"

"One of them was outside the door and knocked out Bernie," Stuart, replied nervously. "He got Bernie's remote and opened the door." Winston almost became unhinged at that; however, he remained calm, his exterior showing no reaction.

"That will be all," Winston said, glancing dismissively at the three. "Oh, did you go through decontamination before coming down here?" Stuart nodded.

"Are the two guards and Bernie in isolation?"

"Yes."

"Last of all, is a new guard stationed outside the entrance?" One last nod and Winston waved them away.

He leaned back in his chair and sighed. "We are so close." He murmured to himself. He gazed at the picture on the wall of his father, taken before the disaster. Smiling, dark thick hair, so like his, blowing in the ocean breeze on a windy day at the beach. He looked tanned and healthy, tall and lean. He and his brother, Terrence, were younger, though paler versions of him. As if thinking about his brother conjured him up, the door suddenly flew open. Terrence strode into the room, gray eyes, so like his own, blazing like hot iron.

"When were you planning on telling me about the breech?" he yelled. "I need to know what is going on at all times."

"Sit down," Winston pointed to the chair in front of his desk. "And close that door."

Terrence glared at his brother, then turned around and closed the door, standing in front of it, arms crossed. Winston stared at him, his eyes growing steely cold. Terrence sat down.

"First of all, I just found out myself. Everything is under control." Winston leaned forward to emphasize his

130

point. "All decontamination protocol was followed. We are safe."

Terrence leaped up and began pacing. "We have to act now. Our security is at risk. After this incident, the outside world will know of our existence and it's just a matter of time until those barbarians out there will be at our door."

"It's too soon," Winston replied. "Our brothers have just reached maturity. They must be protected until they are fully prepared. They are our hope for the future."

An unnatural silver glint shown in Terrence's eyes, "We were the first, you and I." He smiled widely, but it did not reach his cold gray eyes.

Winston nodded in agreement. "That is why we are the natural leaders of Residuum. Our father had a plan for the future. We are an integral part of that plan. Now, you need to maintain your calm. We mustn't worry our constituents. They depend on us for guidance."

Terrence laughed. "That's funny, our constituents. But you're right. We need them in order to succeed. At least for now," he added.

"Yes, they are mere chattel, but they don't know that. They are working for the greater cause, after all." Winston chuckled. "We must keep them believing that. Soon we will escape this underground prison and join the world out there, on our own terms, of course."

"Of course," Terrence agreed wholeheartedly.

"Furthermore," he continued, "this small matter of two uncouth, brainless lowbrows entering our facility is not important. They accomplished their mission of procuring the woman. After escaping, they were probably fornicating as soon as they were out the door." Terrence laughed, amused at his brother's uncharacteristic use of vulgarity.

"Now will you check on the progress of Professor Rowland and Doctor Lane?" Winston smoothly changed the direction of the conversation. "It's essential we keep them happy, at least until they complete their part of the project."

"Last time I talked to the professor, he said they were processing the last ingredients," Terrence answered, standing up to go. "And he wasn't very pleasant about it either. I'll be glad when I don't have to kiss his ass anymore."

"Yes, soon he will have served his purpose," Winston agreed. "For now, please keep me updated on his progress. Without his successful contribution to our plan, all will be in vain."

Chapter Twenty Two

Elizabeth didn't know how long she lay there. The throbbing had lessened considerably, leaving a dull ache. She felt the back of her head, feeling a small lump in the area of her original head injury. Grabbing the towels on the floor, she wiped up the water on the floor and nightstand. Rising slowly to her feet, she sat on the edge of the bed, trying to gain control of her emotions. With her memories returning, her feelings were all tangled up inside her like a knot.

Elizabeth glanced at the clock on the nightstand. It was about an hour after sunrise. She decided to dress and go out to the cabin. She had no appetite. Maybe she would grab some tea from the cupboard and make a cup to relax her, although she didn't think anything could accomplish that.

Once in the cabin, she heated water on the stove, poured it over the tea bag in her cup and sat down at the table, distractedly swirling the hot liquid with a spoon. The morning sun blazed in the eastern sky. Lost in her thoughts, she didn't hear Merlin enter until he cleared his throat behind her.

Turning, she smiled a greeting.

"Mind if I join you?" he asked.

"Not at all," she beckoned toward the other chair.

"Tanner hasn't returned yet," Merlin said in concern, sitting down at the table.

"Oh? Elizabeth said, distractedly. So caught up in her thoughts, she had forgotten about his mission. "When were you expecting them back?"

"Before sunrise, at least I was hoping."

"Merlin, I need to talk to you," Elizabeth began.

"Yes, dear?"

"This morning I slipped and fell," she said. Concern etched Merlin's face. "I hit my head again and somehow it helped me regain my memories. I know who I am."

Knowing Merlin, she wasn't surprised when he immediately got up and asked if he could look at her injury. She nodded and pointed to the back of her head.

He gently prodded and closely peered until satisfied. "It's a small bump. For that, I'm relieved." He sat back down.

"Now, you say the injury caused you to regain your lost memories?"

She nodded. "Yes, as a matter of fact..." A commotion drew her eyes to the window. Tweeny appeared, followed by Laden with Tanner bringing up the rear, carrying a woman. Elizabeth stared in disbelief. Merlin, seeing them also, jumped up to open the door.

They stumbled into the cabin. Tweeny headed toward the entrance to the cave. "I'm starved. Laden?"

"I'm right behind you." They bolted for the hidden door. "Tanner will fill you in."

"Thanks," he yelled as he lay the woman down on the bed in the other room, Merlin right behind him.

"You are making a habit of rescuing women in need," Merlin commented, glancing at Elizabeth.

"We found her in the mountain." He paused, eyeing Merlin. "Cheyenne Mountain."

"What did you say?" Merlin stared in disbelief at Tanner "There's people still alive there?"

"Yes. They control the night stalkers. They use them to obtain slaves." As Merlin was examining the woman, Tanner told them what happened in the mountain and how they managed to free the woman from certain captivity and then they escaped.

Merlin hesitated in his examination of the woman. "There are people living there. Then maybe Vivien is...it's possible she could be alive somewhere in that mountain." Hopeful eyes held Tanner's.

"Now Merlin, we don't know if..."

Interrupting him from the doorway, Elizabeth whispered, "Merlin, your wife is alive." She stood frozen, looking bewildered at her own words.

Tanner's entire body went cold. He advanced toward Elizabeth. "That's enough," he warned. "How could you possibly know anything about that?"

"I know because…" she hesitated.

"She knows because, her memory has come back," Merlin finished for her. His eyes burned with hopeful intensity. Tanner's blazed with incredulity. Elizabeth, realizing the truth of her words, stood her ground.

Tanner crossed his arms over his chest and shook his head. "Merlin, can you please explain to me exactly what's happened since I've been gone, what, all of one night?" He threw a pointed look at Merlin. "Every time I leave, I come back to some crazy story."

"First, I need to stabilize our patient here. You two go out there and talk. I'll be out soon."

Grumbling, Tanner followed Elizabeth out the door.

"Would you like some tea?" she quietly asked.

"No, I don't want…" Tanner began. Suddenly all the anger drained out of him and a profound weariness settled in. "Tea sounds fine, thank you." He fell heavily onto the chair. "Give me Merlin's special concoction. It's hidden in the back of the cupboard."

Elizabeth found a canister marked "special occasions" and held it up. "Yeah, that's the one" Tanner said. "I need all the help I can get to understand the conversation we're about to have. I wasn't planning on tea and a chat when I got home." He slouched with fatigue.

136

Her mind whirling, Elizabeth managed to fix the tea and set a cup in front of him, noticing for the first time how drained and exhausted he looked. She replenished her cup with the new tea. She probably needed the special brew as much as Tanner and didn't look forward to what might become an interrogation. And she wasn't sure how much she should tell him.

Noticing Elizabeth's wary look, Tanner said, "I just want to know what's going on. I don't want to get Merlin's hopes up, but if what you say is true then we have got a real problem here. My grandmother, Vivien, would not willing stay away for twenty years without at least sending us a message that she was well." Wearily, Tanner closed his eyes.

"She is well and she did send a message…with me," Elizabeth stated. Tanner's eyes flew open.

Incredulous, he sat up straight and momentarily studied her, "You're serious?"

"I've never been more serious in my life."

"Who exactly are you?"

"My um… my name is Elizabeth Rowland. My father is Professor Albert Rowland. He is an astrophysicist in Cheyenne Mountain. He was the leader of the TAG wave field project."

"And he and Vivien worked together on the project, till the very end," Merlin added, standing quietly in the doorway. His eyes took on a faraway look. "I met him once, you know, when I visited Vivien. They were so hopeful." He shook his head. "I think I need some of that tea, also."

Merlin closed the door to the bedroom and walked over to the stove to prepare his cup of tea. Tanner stared at

137

Elizabeth who was studying the bottom of her cup. Merlin sat down with his tea, and as if sudden realization hit him, grabbed Elizabeth's hands, his eyes shining brightly. "She's alive? She's really alive?"

"Yes, Merlin." Elizabeth laughed, tears threatening to start. "She really is alive. I was with her right before I left Cheyenne Mountain and she sent a message with me to deliver to you."

Merlin wiped at his tears. "A message? But where is it. There was no message on you when we found you."

"I know," she looked at Tanner. "You have to take me back where you found me. It's there. I hid it. It's the last thing I remember."

Chapter Twenty Three

Tanner sat staring, unable to comprehend Elizabeth's words. He stood, measuring her with his eyes. "You hid it? You're not making any sense." He paused, at a loss for words.

"For Merlin's sake I am going to go along with this. But, I'm not going anywhere right now. As entertaining as all this is, I can barely keep my eyes open."

"He's right," Merlin said, seeing the exhaustion in Tanner's body. "He's been up all night. It will have to wait until he's had some sleep."

"Right now, I am going to get a bite to eat and then I'll be zonked out in my room."

"Yes, of course," Elizabeth said. "I didn't mean right this minute." She also needed time. Time to figure out how much information to reveal.

Tanner gazed at her, as if he knew what she was thinking. He started to say something, shook his head and walked out of the cabin. Elizabeth relaxed. The interrogation would come later. She would be more prepared after she was able to organize her thoughts. Her mind still roiled with disjointed memories, many of them confusing and uncomfortable.

"Merlin, can we talk later? My head hurts and I need to rest. I couldn't sleep last night and now my mind is a jumble."

"I understand, dear. Thank you. I am overjoyed just knowing Vivien is alive. We will have plenty of time to talk later." The sadness that always seemed a part of him had lifted. Elizabeth nodded, smiling softly at Merlin as she rose to go.

Merlin sat at the table sipping his tea, lost in his memories when he heard a blood-curling scream come from the bedroom. He lurched forward, spilling his tea. Jumping up, he rushed to the room.

139

His new patient was sitting in the middle of the bed. Her matted hair partially covered her face. She was brandishing one of the sharp instruments he had unthinkingly left on the nightstand.

"Don't come near me," she screamed. Terror etched across her face.

Merlin raised his hands. Gently he said, "I'm a doctor. I am here to help you."

Unconvinced, she spat out, "You're with the night stalkers. They captured me and brought me to their…to their lair."

"No, dear. We rescued you from them. You're safe now."

Something about Merlin's tone seemed to have a calming effect on her. Peering at Merlin through strands of dirty hair, she lowered the instrument, her eyes still wary. Glancing beyond him through the doorway, she saw a cozy kitchen and light shining through a window.

"Where am I?" she asked cautiously.

"You're at the Manitou Colony. You were rescued last night and brought here."

Relief swept through her. Could she be so lucky? She silently looked around the room. "I've heard of this colony, good things too."

"Yes, well, we take care of the people here and try to help those in need." He nodded in the direction of her hand. "If you don't mind, can I have that back?"

Hesitating a moment as she studied Merlin, she finally held the instrument out and Merlin gently took it from her shaky hand and put it back in his bag.

140

"What's your name, dear?"

"Cara. My name's Cara."

"Where did you live? Before you were captured."

"I was helping Doc Reynolds at the mutant camp. I heard the night stalkers didn't go near the camp, so I felt safe there."

"The mutant camp?" Merlin enquired.

"Yeah, on the river, south of the burnt out camp."

"I know of it. In fact, Doctor Reynolds is an old friend of mine. How are things going at the camp?"

"As well as can be expected. We have built a few buildings and grow some crops. The river is teaming with fish."

"How were you captured?"

"I was too far from camp when it got dark. They surprised me. I fought them, but there were too many of them."

"Well, you're safe now," Merlin patted her hand and got up. "Why don't you rest and I'll be back in a little while to check on you. Are you hungry?" Cara nodded.

"I'll get you some food. The bathroom is over there if you want to clean up. There's a brush and comb on the shelf." Merlin left, closing the door behind him with a soft click.

Unsuccessfully trying to thread her fingers through her matted hair, Cara gave up and lay back, casually taking in her surroundings with a smile. The irony of the situation did not escape her. This was the very place she had been headed for when she was captured. She hadn't been totally honest with Merlin. And now, through the unintentional help of the night stalkers, she was right where she wanted to be. She put her hand to her mouth to stifle a laugh threatening to erupt.

In due time, Merlin returned with a tray of food from the dining hall. He knocked softly and entered. Cara was sitting up against the backboard, her face scrubbed clean and her dark blonde hair combed and pulled back away from her face.

Now that Merlin could clearly see her, she looked to be in her early thirties. Her face had been hardened from the sun and the harsh environment of the last twenty years. She had a lean hungry look about her. Trying to survive in the outside world did that to a person.

"Here you go, dear," Merlin set the tray on the bed. Her eyes widened at the fresh biscuits and eggs. Needing no prompting, she ravenously ate everything on the plate.

Once finished she leaned back against the pillows. "Sorry about my manners. That was delicious."

"I understand," Merlin said, taking the tray and setting it on the small table by the bed. "You need to gather your strength. Food and rest is what you need."

"Thank you Merlin." With a full belly, she was becoming drowsy, her eyes heavy.

"I am going to let you get some rest now," Merlin said as he grabbed the tray and turned to go. "We'll talk later about what your plans are." Cara nodded as she sunk heavily into the pillows, and she was already fast asleep when Merlin quietly closed the door.

Chapter Twenty Four

Elizabeth was able to rest for a couple of hours. Although still exhausted, her mind was too wound up to relax so she got up. Going to the dining hall for lunch, she decided to stop by the medical facilities to see Jom. When she entered, he was sitting up laughing at something Laden had said. Raini was there too.

"Hi," Elizabeth said smiling. "You look much better today."

"Feeling better too," Jom said. "Laden was telling us about his adventure in Cheyenne Mountain. Merlin was right. People are really in there."

Elizabeth stiffened. The last thing she wanted to talk about was Cheyenne Mountain. "Yes, so I heard." She glanced around the room. "I was headed to the dining hall. Does anyone need anything?"

If they were curious about her abruptness, no one said anything. "I'm fine. I just ate," Jom replied and waved his hand at Laden and Raini. "I think these two are going that way."

"We want to sit with you for a while longer Jom," Raini said. "We'll see you down there in a little bit, Elizabeth." She smiled shyly at Laden who returned the smile.

Elizabeth saw the exchange and the way Raini looked at Laden. With sudden realization she knew that Raini really liked Laden and from his looks, it was more than likely mutual. Although it was hard to see his eyes through the goggles, she was sure he was gazing at Raini in the same way. Elizabeth felt an upsurge of happiness at the thought. Waving goodbye, she smiled to herself.

After eating lunch, Elizabeth walked to the rec. room. On her way, she passed Tanner's room. There was a 'do not disturb' sign on the door. He had drawn a skull and cross

144

bones under it. Elizabeth chuckled. She certainly wasn't about to disturb him.

There were a few people scattered around the room. An old movie was playing, but nobody was paying much attention to it. All the talk was on Cheyenne Mountain. Word had gotten around. She needed to talk to Merlin and Tanner as soon as Tanner woke up. There was so much to tell them but would they believe her? She could barely believe it herself.

That evening, Elizabeth went searching for Merlin and Tanner. She found Tanner in the dining hall, but Merlin was not around.

"He's actually in the medical center," Tanner explained to her inquiry concerning his whereabouts. "Angie, Shelton's wife, went into labor earlier. Merlin is helping with the delivery. It looks like we'll have a new addition to our colony soon." His eyes showed a combination of happiness and anxiety.

Elizabeth knew the high mortality rates of women and children in today's world and understood Tanner's anxiety. She hoped everything went well for both mother and baby. An image of another pregnant woman invaded her mind, stomach grossly bloated, wrists tied to the bed, pleading silently with her eyes.

"Well?" Tanner was looking at her strangely.

"Excuse me? Sorry, I didn't hear the question. I was distracted."

"No kidding. You were in another world."

"Yes, another world," she said quietly.

Tanner studied Elizabeth for a moment. "I asked if you wanted to explain all this…this return of your memory stuff. Here is as good a place as any. It's pretty quiet this time of night."

Elizabeth looked around. Gertie was at the counter cleaning up. Everyone else had left. "Yes this is fine," she replied, with a sigh. "The problem is I really don't know where to start."

"The beginning, perhaps?"

Elizabeth threw him a look. Tanner grinned, clearly enjoying himself. He wasn't going to make this easy on her.

Taking a moment to gather her thoughts, she began, "As you now know, there's people in Cheyenne Mountain."

Tanner nodded. "They're not particularly pleasant, either."

"I was inside the mountain twenty years ago when it was bombed. I was only six at the time and I knew something had gone dreadfully wrong. Of course later I found out about the failure of the lunar project and the disastrous consequences for the earth. With all the reinforcements built into the mountain, only a small portion was destroyed as well as the main entrance, which caved in, piling up tons of rocks."

Elizabeth hesitated before continuing. "It proved to be an impossible task to remove them. We had no way out, but we were prepared for this kind of emergency. We had supplies to last many, many years, botanical gardens and an underground reservoir we could tap into. To generate our power, we had a stockpile of rare earth elements and the technical knowhow to convert them into energy. We also had

146

instruments to measure the radiation levels outside and understood we couldn't go out anyway."

Elizabeth paused, "Spencer Shell was in charge of operations. Everything ran pretty smoothly at first. I was pretty sheltered and protected and spent most of my time in my father's lab. He taught me everything he knew about astrophysics."

"Ah, the book you were reading."

"Excuse me?"

"I noticed the book you were reading when you first got here. I was curious. That explains it."

"Oh. Anyway, about five years ago, Spencer passed away, leaving his sons in charge. Suddenly, everything changed. We were all forced to have GPS chips implanted in our arms and there were sections of the facility that were now off limits, with guards at the door. We heard rumors that two smaller entrances had been tunneled out, one on the north side, the one you found, and another one on the south side. However, we were told there was still no way to get outside."

"It seems, you went from being sheltered to being captives," Tanner commented.

Elizabeth nodded. "Yes, that's exactly how we felt. Vivien, complained vehemently to my father that she wanted to return home to her family and she believed there was a way out."

"Vivien, my grandmother." It was more a statement than a question.

"Yes, we have grown very close over the years."

"Oh." He looked at her questioningly, searching her eyes, seeking the truth in her words. Sighing deeply he said,

"You know what? I'm beginning to actually believe this wild story of yours might be true."

"Thank you," Elizabeth said with relief. "Your grandmother has told me so much about you and Merlin, though she didn't mention how stubborn you were."

"It's been twenty years. I was just a nine-year old kid the last time I saw her. Stubbornness is a virtue I've acquired over the years."

Elizabeth smiled and the mood lightened momentarily before she continued. "Vivien was working on a way to get out of the mountain without the knowledge of the Shell brothers. They were gaining more control; creating a new government they called Residuum. We were forced to pledge our allegiance to them. They believed we needed a strong unified front when we eventually got out of the mountain because the world was dangerous."

"Well, they were right about that."

"Then we heard new rumors. We heard the government was performing procedures on individuals to change their genetic makeup and control their minds."

"The night stalkers?"

"Probably, though I never saw them. But, it was more than that. Residuum was engineering biotechnology in infants, implanting atomic computerized chips to enhance their intellect. It was kept under wraps and under very tight security."

Stopping to gather her thoughts, Elizabeth continued. "Pop, that's my father, heard rumors about some kind of brotherhood Spencer created, some sort of elite group. No one knows much about it. Supposedly, his sons, Winston and

148

Terrence, were the first to have the neural implants when they were infants. As the story goes, Spencer's early experiments were on them."

"A new concept for fatherly love."

"That's not all," Elizabeth continued. They have a fertilization clinic to impregnate women to create babies they can train for specific jobs. The newborns are called the generic group as opposed to the elite group. With a large supply of frozen embryos, all they needed were women to implant them in. After learning about the night stalkers, I believe they used them to steal women."

"Now that I think about it, more women than men have gone missing in the past," mused Tanner.

"The clinic isn't kept under such strict security as the brotherhood, so I made it past a guard and saw women and girls in cells."

Elizabeth hesitated, swallowing hard. "They were strapped to their beds, their bellies huge. I believe they were impregnating them with four or five embryos at once and multiple babies were born from each woman. Many of them were not grown women. They were young girls, barely in their teens. They force people to work in the nurseries and they keep impregnating the same women and girls. Residuum wants to repopulate the earth, but with their own people whom they can control."

Incredulous with the idea, Tanner's eyes widened in shock. "They probably created the night stalkers first when they realized they needed more females," he said thoughtfully. "Then they used them to abduct women and girls for fertilization and men and boys for whatever jobs they required of them. We first came into contact with the night stalkers about five years ago, so that fits the timeline of when Spencer Shell died."

"And now, Winston and Terrence plan to open up the mountain and break out of their self-made prison. Cheyenne Mountain is a huge underground facility and Winston has an armed force of probably at least a thousand men."

"That doesn't seem like a lot, but since we have barely scraped together a hundred men, and we're the largest settlement in the area, we are definitely going to be outnumbered."

"They are also well armed." Tanner frowned at that piece of information.

"The funny thing is Winston and Terrence are obsessively fearful of contamination from the outside world, but with their manpower, and their technology, they plan on taking control of the whole area. Whether they actually go outside is debatable."

"How ironic. They plan on taking over the world, but are too scared to come out of hiding." Tanner laughed, but there was no amusement in his voice.

"We realized we needed help if we were to succeed in stopping them. Terrence was always telling me he had a secret weapon and then he would laugh hysterically. Sometimes I think that implant has affected his mind, and not in a positive way."

"Do you think he might be psychologically unstable?"

"Perhaps." Elizabeth didn't want to talk about Terrence and wished she hadn't brought him up. "Anyway, we made careful plans for my escape. I was to find you and Merlin. Vivien was sure you had survived. I was to explain the situation and ask for your help."

"To escape Cheyenne Mountain? Of course we'll help."

"No, not to escape, at least not yet." Elizabeth hesitated. "I need supplies. I have to go back."

"Go back! Are you out of you mind?" Tanner yelled. Gertie looked up from wiping the counter. He lowered his voice and leaned forward. "You can't go back."

"I have to. There's something I need to finish. It's important…for everyone."

"What is so important you have to return to that viper's den?"

"I can't…it's difficult to explain." She stood up. "I will show you."

Elizabeth headed down the tunnel toward the cabin. When they reached it, she opened the door and took his hand to lead him outside. He could feel her trembling hand, cool to the touch.

They walked to the clearing just outside the cabin. Hours ago, the sun had cast its last tendril across the evening sky; the heavens now bathed in a richness of brilliant stars. Still holding his hand, she stopped to carefully study the night sky then pointed to the west.

"Do you see over there? It looks like a bright star just above the horizon?"

He looked where she pointed. "Yes," Tanner replied. "That's one of the planets; at least, I think it is. You would know more about that than me." He smiled down at her, enjoying the unexpected closeness.

She returned his smile, looking back at the distant bright point of light. "Tanner, that's the moon."

Chapter Twenty Five

Tanner blinked at Elizabeth once, twice. He slowly let go of her hand and gazed at the western sky not saying a word. The silence was deafening, his expression inscrutable.

"I know it's hard to believe, but I can explain," Elizabeth began hesitantly.

"I'm listening," said Tanner, without so much as a flicker of a glance in her direction, still gazing at the night sky.

Elizabeth drew in a massive breath. "When my father realized what was happening to the moon, he shut the anti-gravity field down. He managed to do it before the moon was totally flung out of earth's gravity field. It is still out there, revolving around us, but too far away to exert much of an influence on the earth."

Tanner stood very still as if unable to move.

Elizabeth continued. "We have been working on the anti-gravity field for the last ten years. At first, we thought it was hopeless, that we could not generate enough energy to create the field again."

She glanced cautiously at Tanner who remained deadly silent. "We have been able to engineer the rare-earth elements needed and are now able to generate a weak field. We are missing three minerals necessary to create a strong enough anti-gravity field. I left Cheyenne Mountain because Vivien said your colony had a stockpile of these minerals and I came here to enlist your help in obtaining them."

Tanner finally turned and looked at her.

"I need to return with these minerals, so we can generate a field strong enough to return the moon to its original orbit around the earth. At least that is what we hope to do." She looked into his face with an air of expectancy, unsure of his reaction to this startling news.

Tanner gazed at her for a weighty moment, his stony countenance gradually changing to a look of utter amazement, as if he just realized what she had said. Then he threw back his head and howled with laughter.

"Well, I hardly believe it's a laughing matter," Elizabeth grumbled. "This is not a joke. I'm entirely serious."

"Oh, Elizabeth," Tanner said, wiping his eyes. "That's just it, I do believe you. What would be the purpose of fabricating a lie like that? All this time the moon has been up there and no one knew. That's the joke." Elizabeth gasped as Tanner caught her up in his arms and swung her around, laughing. She couldn't help but join in his merriment.

He set her down, his arms still around her. "We need to talk to Merlin, of course. I know he'll agree to help you in any way we can. However, there is one stipulation. You're not going back to that mountain alone."

She slowly slipped out of his arms and stepped back. "I will not jeopardize your lives any more than I already have."

Tanner ignored her and began pacing, intermittently stopping to look up at the point of light on the horizon, shaking his head, pacing again. She grabbed his arm. "Listen to me. We had it all planned out. After we returned the moon to its orbit, we were going to make our break."

"Well, now you have help," stated Tanner. "Elizabeth, if you want our help, then you have to agree to the terms. You are not going in there alone."

Elizabeth knew by his look that he was not going to give in on this. "Okay, we don't have time to argue about it, but we do need a plan. You can't just go in there with guns blazing. Operation Moonshine is our first priority."

"Operation Moonshine?" Tanner raised his brows in questioning amusement. "That's what you call this serious endeavor to return the moon to its orbit and save the earth and humanity from a deluge of unprecedented proportions?"

"Yes that's what we call it," Elizabeth answered in irritation. "One night Pop and Vivien drank too much of our distilled alcohol and by the end of that jolly night they had

154

come up with the name as a joke, but it stuck. Not making light of the seriousness of the situation, this is what we call it."

Tanner sobered. "Alright, Operation Moonshine it is. Let's go find Merlin."

After taking one last look at the western sky, they returned to the cabin. Closing the door behind him, Tanner said, "We will need time to plan if we're to be successful in getting into Cheyenne Mountain."

"Time is something I don't have. I must get the minerals and return as soon as possible. I'm sure Pop and Vivien are nearly out of their minds with worry."

In the other room of the cabin, Cara jumped up quickly when she heard voices and quietly hurried to the door to listen in on their conversation. Their voices were soon cut off as they entered the cave, but she had heard enough.

She returned to her bed, deep in thought. What an interesting bit of news. The rumor is true; there are people in Cheyenne Mountain and Tanner is planning on attacking it. She smiled to herself; this changes everything.

Chapter Twenty Six

It seemed too quiet in the medical facility. Elizabeth and Tanner stepped in the main room and looked around. Jom was sleeping peacefully in his room; the door to the maternity section was closed. Without warning, the door opened and out stepped Shelton looking worn out.

"Is everything alright," asked Elizabeth.

Shelton glanced up and smiled broadly. "Angie had the baby. She's fine and the baby's fine. A girl and she is healthy looking. Merlin checked her over and couldn't find any apparent defects."

"That's great news," said Tanner, shaking Shelton's hand.

"Can we see the baby, or is it too soon?" asked Elizabeth as she gave Shelton a quick hug.

"Merlin's still in there cleaning up, maybe a little later."

"Okay," said Tanner. "Will you tell Merlin we need to talk to him as soon as he's finished? Tell him it's important. We'll be in the library."

Shelton nodded. "I'm heading off to get some food. I'll see you later."

Tanner and Elizabeth went back out to the main tunnel and turned toward the library. Walking along quietly, keeping to their own thoughts, Elizabeth broke the silence, "Tanner, we have to go back to where you found me. I have important information there."

"We'll go first thing tomorrow." They entered the library and, finding a comfortable looking couch, sat down. "What exactly is so important? Don't you know the rare earth minerals that you need?"

"Yes. It's not just that." Hesitating, she looked at him with apprehension.

"Oh no. I know that look. Just get it out. We can worry about my reaction later."

"Well, it concerns how I got here."

"Yes, I've been wondering that. How did you get here?"

"Yes, I've been curious about that also," came a voice from the doorway. They looked up to see Merlin. He quickly pulled up a chair to join them.

"Oh, hi Merlin." Elizabeth smiled. "Are Angie and the baby alright?"

"Yes. Angie was a real trooper and the baby is doing just fine." Looking at them both expectantly, he asked, "Now what have I missed?"

Tanner just shook his head. "It's a long story, Merlin and one you'll have a hard time believing. Crazy as this sounds, the moon didn't hurl out in to space. It is still up there, though considerably farther away."

Merlin's shocked expression said it all. "What?"

"Yes, you heard me right. And this is the best part. Elizabeth's father and Grandma have been working on the TAG wave and have figured out a way to create the field again and possibly bring the moon back to its orbit."

"That is unbelievable."

"The problem is they need some rare earth minerals and Elizabeth was sent here to get them. She needs to bring them back in order to power the magnetic fields and make it strong enough for the field to work."

"We do have a stock pile on the lower level. I just need to know what you need."

"Vivien wrote a list and sent a note for you two," said Elizabeth. "We are going back to get it tomorrow. There is something else I need, too. It concerns how I got here and how I'm returning." She hesitated.

"Yes?" Tanner prodded as they both looked at her expectantly.

"Once again I'm at a loss for words," Elizabeth frowned then continued. "Basically, I flew here."

"What?" They both exclaimed simultaneously.

"Here we go again," Tanner shook his head. Then he smiled wryly, encouraging her to go on.

158

"Okay, Vivien has also been working on another project in her spare time. We call it Project Icarus."

"Do you mean the Icarus of legend who flew too close to the sun, despite his father's warning, and melted his wings and fell to the earth?" Tanner asked.

"Yes. Only these wings don't melt. "I literally flew out of the side of the mountain where our lab opens up to the outside."

"Do the leaders know you're gone," Merlin asked.

"No." Elizabeth held up her arm. "Vivien removed the tracking device from my arm. When I crash landed, I tore open the wound and hit my head."

"How are they keeping your whereabouts a secret?"

"They are using the chip. They put it on a human sized robot with a hazmat suit during work hours and move it around in the evening. At night, they put it in my bed and lock the door. We all thought I would be back within a week. I must get back. It could already be too late. Winston and Terrence may have become suspicious and demanded to see me."

"Okay, tomorrow we'll take a hike and try to find the location. We'll leave early in the morning, around sunrise." Tanner stood up. "Now, I'm heading to my room and I'm going to try to get some sleep." He shook his head. "The moon is really…"

Elizabeth just nodded. "Thank you Tanner." He waved his farewell.

Merlin smiled at Elizabeth. "So Vivien is doing well?"

"Yes, very much so. She is feisty and has helped me out so many times I've lost count."

"You know, I've never given up hope that somehow she survived. Knowing she's truly alive, well…" Merlin choked back a sob.

Elizabeth squeezed his hand. "I know."

Merlin cleared his throat and stood. "Well, I must get back to work. I need to check on Angie and the baby before I retire. I will see you tomorrow."

"Good night," said Elizabeth as she followed him out of the library.

The next morning Tanner and Elizabeth walked along the trail heading back to where Tanner had discovered Elizabeth. The sun having just risen, bathed the forest in bright light. It was still cool with a morning breeze ruffling the trees. Tanner knew he could have gone on his own and brought the wings back without Elizabeth. He didn't want to admit that he enjoyed her companionship.

"How long of a hike is it?" Elizabeth asked, stepping over a large branch blocking the trail.

"It should take about an hour to get there. We'll pass through the upper part of old Manitou Springs. The trail head is on the other side."

"I was so young, I can barely remember the town. I know, we visited a candy shop and I got a special treat."

"There's not much there anymore. Most of it was swept away in flood after flood. There's a few buildings still standing that were farther from the river. Now the river has almost dried up. With the temperatures getting warmer,

160

there is very little snowfall during the winter, so not much run off. It's October and it's much hotter than the Octobers I remember when I was young.

"If project moonshine works, the earth's orbit will begin to stabilize again from the gravitational pull of the returned moon. Earth will regain its tilt and we'll once again have seasons."

"And the oceans will recede?" He looked at her questioningly.

"Yes. The oceans will recede and the polar ice caps will once again trap water as ice, hopefully before the water reaches us. I really don't know how long it will take for the earth to return to its prior climate."

"You know, since you've been here, you have tipped our world upside down." Tanner smiled. "I mean that in a good way."

Elizabeth smiled back. "I know what you mean. First, I fly off, not knowing what to expect, then I lose my memory, and now I am returning home more hopeful than I have been in a long time. I just hope Pop and Vivien have not given up on me."

Chapter Twenty Seven

"You must wake up." Professor Albert Rowland gently patted Doctor Vivien Lane's arm. "You can't sleep here in the lab, Vivien. Go to your room and get a good night's rest. Please?"

Vivien groggily raised her head and blinked. "Oh, I did it again." She stretched her arms and took a gulp of the coffee, now cold, on the lab table. Grimacing, she nonetheless took another drink before sitting it down. "I was going over the numbers again."

Vivien looked up into the kind, worried eyes of the professor. He was the picture of the stereotypical professor, with his oversized glasses and gray hair in disarray. She couldn't help but notice how weathered his face had become and the sleep-deprived circles that cut under his eyes.

"We need to be prepared when Elizabeth returns," Vivien murmured, as she once again went over her notes. The professor studied her for a moment. Her brown hair, pulled back in a braid, had slowly taken on gray strands over the years and the contrasting colors wove through the braid. She reflected a quiet dignity, and her face, though aged, was still pretty, her eyes intelligent.

Sitting down beside her, Albert took her hand in his and squeezed gently. "You know we are prepared."

She turned to Albert. "We should never have let her go. "It's just too dangerous out there." A shiver ran through her slim body.

"She was insistent and she was the only one who could leave for an extended amount of time without being missed."

"But it's been almost two weeks and we've heard nothing from her."

"I know. Believe me, I'm as worried as you are."

"Fortunately," Vivien began, "we have been able to hide her absence so far when we removed the chip from her arm, but Terrence is going to get suspicious if she doesn't show herself pretty soon."

Lowering her voice, she continued, "Yesterday I told him she had been exposed to a radioactive compound in one of the rare earth minerals and is in decontamination. Then she will be quarantined for three days as an extra precaution. As paranoid as he and his brother are of being contaminated, he left pretty quickly without an argument."

They heard footsteps approaching. Exchanging concerned looks, they turned to see Terrence Shell step into the lab.

"Still at work, huh?" He asked with his usual smirk in place. "You two seem to be working around the clock, yet you're still not ready."

"The process must be precise or it won't work," Professor Rowland replied.

"So you've said." Terrence glanced around the lab. "I assume Elizabeth is still in the decontamination unit of the lab." The professor nodded.

"Very well. As soon as she is out of quarantine, I want her to report to my office." Not awaiting an answer, he turned on his heel and left, his footsteps echoing down the quiet hall.

Albert and Vivien stared at each other in growing concern. They didn't know how much longer they could stall. If Winston and Terrence knew Elizabeth had left Cheyenne Mountain without their permission, they would be livid and suspicious.

"What are we going to do if Elizabeth isn't back in three days?" Vivien asked, her frown deepening. "We are running out of excuses."

"I know. We'll have to tell them the truth or some version of it. They won't hurt us because they need us. But if she doesn't return with what we need, this project will surely fail."

After leaving the lab, Terrence's expression immediately darkened. A flash of anger crossed his face; he knew they were keeping something from him, but what? The GPS computer grid showed everyone was in his or her correct location.

He took the elevator down into the depths of the mountain to the highest security level. The door opened and guards stood before the entrance to the technical center of the whole complex, the computer brain that controlled it all. Barely glancing at the guards, he went in and sat down in front of the GPS grid, checking the various levels and everyone's whereabouts.

The professor and doctor were still in the lab. It looked like the computer geek Norman had joined them. That wasn't unusual. There was Elizabeth in quarantine just like they said. He still had a prickling at the back of his neck.

Someone cleared his throat behind him and Terrence jumped.

"A little apprehensive are we?" An amused voice inquired. "What has got you on edge, brother?"

"Don't sneak up behind me like that." Terrence complained, not bothering to turn around.

"Sneak is such a vulgar word." Winston sat down beside him. "Stealth, subterfuge, now those are more appropriate words, more suitable for our purposes."

Terrence grunted, not looking up from the computer grid. "I don't know. I've just got this feeling that things aren't what they seem. Subterfuge alright, but not of our making."

"Oh? Whose subterfuge are we talking about? Remember, we don't gage reality on our feelings, we gage it on our intellect and our superb deductive reasoning."

"I know. It doesn't make sense. Nothing is out of order. I just don't trust the professor and doctor."

"Fortunately for us, that is not an issue. We don't have to trust them. All that is required from them is a successful culmination of their project. After that, they will be expendable."

*   *   *

"Thank you Norm." Vivien sighed. "We'll see you tomorrow." With an expression of concern, Norm waved and left.

Every night at nine Norm arrived at the lab. He was the best computer hacker in the facility. He would turn off the alert on the gateway above them. It would look suspicious if they opened it for a half an hour every evening at nine. The gateway would be opened just wide enough to allow entry. Every night they expectantly waited for Elizabeth's return during the agreed upon half an hour. They had started this routine three days after she left.

"It is getting harder every night," Vivien said as she cleaned the counter tops and prepared to leave. "I don't want to give up hope, but I'm frightened. Elizabeth is all alone out there and if she's hurt or…"

"We have to stay strong," Albert said, as concerned as Vivien. "She's smart. She'll be back."

Vivien looked in his eyes trying to feel a seed of hope. Even though he looked as if he'd aged considerably in the last two weeks, his weary eyes still held a hint of promise in her return.

"What if it was a fool's errand?" Vivien cried. "I don't know if the rest of my family even survived. My son and daughter-in-law were killed before they could get to safety and Tanner was just a young boy the last time I saw him. I have no idea what kind of man he has turned into while having to fight for survival in that world out there."

"I know Vivien, but we mustn't give up hope."

"Oh, Albert, how can this possibly end well? I am so sorry for telling you and Elizabeth about Merlin's building of a nuclear bomb shelter in a cave, giving you hope when there may be none." She turned her head, holding back a sob, and a giant hopelessness opened up inside of her.

Chapter Twenty Eight

"We're getting close," said Tanner, pointing. "I found you near the bottom of the mountain on the trail beside the incline over there." She looked in that direction and saw a crumbling staircase straight up the mountain.

"Wow, did people used to hike that?"

"Yes. It was a challenge for the athletes competing to be in the Olympics. Americans trained here and I guess it was an unwritten rule that they had to make it to the top to be on the team."

"I read about the Olympics. The best athletes in the world competed."

"It seems so long ago," said Tanner. "Most of those athletes, the best of the best, are probably dead now." He shook his head. "Well, we're here at the start of the trail. It winds up alongside the stairway."

They had stopped at an old abandoned parking lot. It was still largely intact with some of the pavement gone, but large sections still remained unscathed. Grass had begun to push up through the cracks and gaps. It was empty of cars; any parked here were long ago swept away by the river.

Elizabeth followed him up the narrow, curving trail. The air was rich with the fragrance of pine. The brilliant rays that had shined hotly from above, heating the parking lot, were now dappled and the air cooler. The path began rising in steep uneven rocky steps. They hadn't gone far when Tanner abruptly stopped in front of a large granite rock sitting on the side of the trail. He pointed to a spot beside it, "I found you here."

Elizabeth glanced around. "I have recollections of falling from the sky, landing hard, then getting up to take off

169

the wings and pack. I stumbled onto the trail and that's the last thing I remember."

"Let's take a look around. Do you know what direction you might have come from?" Elizabeth shook her head.

"In your condition, I doubt if you walked very far. It should be close by."

"It's all kind of hazy." Elizabeth looked around, not recognizing anything.

"First, I'm going to look for broken brush or branches where you might have come through." Tanner began inspecting the area nearby. "Your trail is cold, but we still may find some clues."

After a few minutes, he pointed upward around the rock. "I believe you came from that direction."

Elizabeth nodded and cautiously stepped off the trail, heading upward. It wasn't very level because the trail wound up the side of a mountain. Tanner followed, then they fanned out a little, Tanner always making sure he kept Elizabeth within eyesight.

Off the trail, the terrain was rugged and uneven with thick brush blocking their way at times. They spent an hour combing the steep, jagged terrain above the trail with no results.

"Let's try below the trail," Tanner suggested as he surveyed the area. "This looks like a dead-end."

"I need to rest a minute." Taking out her bottle of water from her small pack, Elizabeth sat wearily on a nearby rock. After taking a drink, she gazed around her. "I wish I could be of more help, but nothing looks familiar."

Sitting on a fallen log, Tanner said, "That's okay. You had just hit your head and you hadn't been outside for twenty years. I think…"

Letting out a yelp, Elizabeth stood up unexpectedly and pointed behind him. "There in the brush, I think I see a part of my back pack." Tanner turned and saw blue fabric showing through the brush.

They hurried over, went around the brush and hidden behind it was a blue pack. Beside the pack, partially hidden, was what looked like layers of feathers attached to a body harness. Elizabeth carefully picked them up and gently shook the dirt out. Tanner could see they were folded in.

"They don't look damaged," said Elizabeth. "I'll carry the wings, if you could please grab the bag." Tanner did and they headed back to the trail.

Once on the trail, Elizabeth stopped, "I need to test the wings and make sure they still work."

"There's the old parking lot."

"Yes, that would work." They followed the winding trail back down until they reached the parking lot. Elizabeth walked to the middle of it and hit a small lever where the harness attached to the wings. The wings opened up.

"They look like large eagle wings," Tanner said in surprise.

"That's because we designed it using the basic wing structure of an eagle." She put on the harness and the wings fit securely on her back with her arms free. On the front of the harness were two small levers. She pointed to one. "This is to raise you up. The higher you push the lever, the higher up you go." She pointed to the other one. "This one gives you

171

forward momentum and you can push it to the right or left to change direction. The wings don't flap. They are stationary. If you catch a thermal you can glide and soar."

"How do you generate the power to lift your weight off the ground?"

"It uses the TAG field. It's just a weaker version."

"So you generate an anti-gravity field around you and up you go."

"Yes, basically that's what happens. I accidentally hit the lever that keeps me up and turned the field off. It was dark and I couldn't see very well, so before I could turn it back on, I crash landed."

She turned and he could see the details of the wings. It was beautiful, about an eight-foot wingspan. There was even a tail that spread out from the bottom of her back.

"Okay, I'm going to give it a try. I hope it still works." She pressed the up lever and quietly began to slowly rise. "It works," she cried. After getting a few feet off the ground, she pressed the other lever and slowly went forward. Going up about twenty feet, she carefully glided around the parking lot and then gently landed in front of Tanner.

"Wow! That was amazing!"

"Would you like to try it?"

"I weigh a lot more than you. Are you sure it will get me off the ground?"

"Yes, I just need to recalibrate it for your weight. How much do you weigh?

"Around one hundred and ninety pounds."

Elizabeth took the wings off and played with a dial at the back of the harness. "There, that should work. Remember the right lever is for up and down and the left lever is for forward motion."

Tanner put the wings on and slowly pulled the right lever up. He immediately began to rise. "Okay, pull up on the other lever and get some forward momentum," Elizabeth called out. He did and zoomed forward. He let up and immediately slowed down. He worked each lever and got higher while moving forward. He curved to the right, soaring in the air, feeling like a giant bird. He headed back to the parking lot and landed a little bumpy in front of Elizabeth.

"That was unbelievable! How much weight do the wings hold?" he asked.

"I don't know, probably quite a lot. Once the field is on, you essentially become weightless."

"Oh yeah? In that case you're coming with me to the top of the incline." He pulled her into his arms.

"Wait a minute." Elizabeth pulled free. "What if you drop me?"

"I won't be very high. It shouldn't hurt too much." Tanner grinned.

"What if I hit my head again and lose my memory?"

"I'll make up a real nice history for you."

Elizabeth laughed. "Hold on. I have a couple extra straps in the pack." She pulled them out and hid the pack in some thick brush. "I'm going to strap myself to the harness, just in case."

"You don't trust me?"

Elizabeth just shook her head, smiling. Tanner grabbed her gently by the shoulders and said, "Elizabeth, I would never drop you." She looked into his warm brown eyes and saw sincerity and something else she couldn't name. She didn't know what to say.

Breaking his intense gaze, Tanner said, "Let me help you with those." He turned her around and pulled the straps tight so she was up against his chest secure.

"Can you reach the levers?" Elizabeth asked.

They begin rising. "That answers that question."

With Tanner's strong arms wrapped around her, Elizabeth felt protected and secure. She liked the feeling. They soared effortlessly to the top of the mountain. Tanner's landing was even better this time. She looked out at the city below her. Even though she knew Colorado Springs had been destroyed, the reality of it took her breath away.

"Dear God." She was speechless. Tanner grabbed her hand.

"I know it's bad, especially the first time you see it. However, we have more urgent problems. Look to the east, on the horizon."

Elizabeth looked and saw a faint blue where prairie should be. "Oh no, the water is approaching." She looked up at him in fear. "I must get back tonight. We are running out of time."

"We need another day to plan. Tomorrow night."

She shivered despite the hot day. "You're right." She looked back at the city. "What is that smoke there and over there?"

He pointed to the north. "That's the academy settlement and to the south over there is the mutant colony."

"The mutant colony?"

174

"Yes. In the years after the destruction, there was a lot of radiation around. Many people were exposed to it. Babies were born with defects and horrible disfigurations. Some were put to death."

Elizabeth gasped. "Doc heard about it and started a camp for parents to bring any babies they didn't want. We began calling it the mutant camp. The people there are mostly gentle folk. They are right in the mind. It's just that their physical defects are hard for some people to accept or even look upon. They are mostly left alone and they seem to get along pretty well with Doc's help. We bring them supplies once a month."

Elizabeth gazed out over the bleak landscape of the ruined city. She realized amidst the despair life was continuing on. The hopeful spirit of humanity hadn't given up. After taking in the view for several more minutes, they decided to fly back down to the parking lot, retrieve the pack and fly back to the cabin.

Rising into the air once again and flying over trees and rocky ridges, Tanner had never felt so free. In the distance, craggy peaks soared upward as if to challenge the sky. Hitting a thermal, they surged upward, yelling out in excitement. Reluctantly, Tanner headed in the direction of the parking lot and carefully levered them down until they were once again touching solid ground.

After un-strapping herself, Elizabeth looked behind Tanner. She stiffened with fear and whispered, "Tanner, there's someone behind you pointing a rifle at us."

Tanner whirled around then let out bark of laughter. "Ben, put that rifle away. You're scaring the little lady here."

175

"Tanner is that you?" A grizzled old man yelled out, lowering his rifle. "I thought you was some big mutant bird. My eyesight ain't what it used to be." He smiled shyly at Elizabeth. "But I know a pretty lady when I see one."

"Elizabeth, meet Ben Wiggins. He lives in a cabin close by and he keeps his eye on the area for us."

"Glad to meet you, Ben. You gave me quite a scare."

"Sorry, miss. I heard some commotion out here and came to investigate." He looked at the wings Tanner had taken off. "That is some strange flying contraption."

"Yes it is," replied Tanner. "And you never saw it, you got that Ben?"

Ben smiled and nodded, a look of shared conspiracy on his face.

"Have you seen any strangers lately?" asked Tanner. "McGee hasn't shown his face around here has he?"

"I haven't seen that rascal since I saw him running so fast I could hardly make out who it was. He was just a blur." Ben cackled with glee. "I'll keep watch, though. Nobody gets by me."

"Thanks Ben." Tanner walked over and shook his hand. "Sorry I don't have time for a visit. We've got to bet back. Keep your eyes open and if you see anything suspicious, let us know." Ben nodded.

Strapping himself back into the harness, Tanner then settled Elizabeth in. She was holding tightly to the pack as they lifted up and away. Ben whooped in astonishment and waved. Waving back, they headed for the cabin, skimming over the trees.

Instead of landing in front of the cabin, Tanner flew to a clearing close by the back entrance and landed. "I don't know much about that woman we rescued, but I feel better going in this way just in case she's up and about. I don't want her seeing anything we can't explain."

*   *   *

Merlin knocked on his patient's door and entered. Cara was sitting up in bed, looking much better.

"How do you feel?"

"I feel great, thank you."

"Your color is better. Let me take your blood pressure and check your heart rate."

As Merlin fussed over his patient, Cara said, "I think I want to go back to the mutant camp tomorrow and talk to Doc. I am sure he's worried about me."

"You look to be in good enough condition," Merlin replied as he put away his instruments. "We can send a rover with you."

"No, I'm fine. I know the area and I'll leave early in the morning. It's about a four-hour journey, and I'll take it easy. I will stay at the camp overnight, so I won't have another run in with night stalkers. I'll come back the following day, if you're sure I'm welcome to live here. I can help wherever you need me."

"I will check with Tanner, but I don't think there should be a problem."

177

"Alright. It's settled then," Cara leaned back against the headboard, contentment relaxing her features.

"Yes," Merlin agreed, standing up. "I will come back later this evening to check on you. If you're still looking and feeling well, I think you will be fine to take your trip."

Merlin closed the door quietly and left. Cara jumped up and began pacing back and forth in the small room. Her earlier look of quiet contentment was replaced by an odd look of glee; mumbling to herself, she began making plans.

Chapter Twenty Nine

The lab was quiet. Terrence Shell looked around, surveying the area quickly with his darting eyes. Everything seemed in its place. He smiled to himself and walked over to the storage facility. Using his key to unlock the door, he entered. Lining the wall on hooks were the wings, so far a total of twelve. He walked over and carefully felt the soft feathers, feeling excitement as well as apprehension at the thought of flying out of their secure dwelling one day. He knew rationally the radiation levels were low enough to be safe, but his fear of contamination could still overwhelm him at times.

"Oh it's you," a voice from the doorway called out. He turned to see Vivien Lane standing there eyeing him curiously. "I saw the door open and wondered who was in here. We don't get many visitors."

"Just checking the wings." He slid his hand away and walked along the wall surveying the others. "Production of them has been stepped up and we will have four more by the end of the week."

"Good. As soon as they arrive, we will attach the batteries and test them."

"No one must test them outside, yet." Terrence frowned. "It's too dangerous."

"Of course."

"Is the Tag field ready?"

"Almost. We just have to synthesize the last of the chemical compounds and we will be ready."

"How do you know it will work?" Terrence asked.

"It worked before. The problem was the timing. Had the meteor not struck the moon before the moon was out of its trajectory, it would have worked." She shook her head sadly. "We were so close."

"Well, this time we have no meteor to worry about. You must time it correctly, you know. We lost many satellites the last time the field was on when they plummeted to the earth. They must not be in the TAG wave field when you generate it. They must be on the other side of the earth."

"We know that." Vivien replied in irritation. "We've been over this many times."

"Just a little reminder," Terrence said, irritation creeping into his voice. Stepping in front of Vivien, he eyed her coldly. "We don't want any mistakes made, now do we?"

Vivien didn't say anything. With a warning glint in his eyes, Terrence brushed passed her and walked out of the storage facility. She could hear his receding footsteps as he left the lab and she breathed a sigh of relief. He always made her feel uncomfortable and she always felt he could see subterfuge and guilt written all over her face. She was not very good at deceit, whereas he was a master of it.

She glanced at the wings lining the wall. Unknown to the Shells, Lou had made two extra. One Elizabeth had and the other was hidden away where the Shells would never find it. They were only aware of the twelve.

"Everything all right?"

Vivien was so lost in her thoughts she hadn't heard the professor step into the room behind her.

"Yes. Terrence just left. He always makes me nervous. He was in here looking at the wings."

180

"All accounted for of course." Albert smiled.

Vivien smiled back. "Of course." Sobering, she said with a sigh, "If Elizabeth doesn't return by tomorrow night, we are going to have some explaining to do. Terrence wants to see her the next day when she gets out of contamination."

"Let's keep our fingers crossed and hope for a miracle."

Chapter Thirty

"I am really going back, and it's really going to work this time," Elizabeth said excitedly as she held the bag of rare-earth elements Merlin had just handed her.

When she and Tanner had returned earlier that day, they had found Merlin and she had given him the letter Vivien had written. With shaking hands, Merlin had read it aloud:

To my Dearest Merlin and Tanner,

I am writing this from the depths of Cheyenne Mountain. Elizabeth is my messenger and she can be trusted completely. Unfortunately, we are being held against our will, so while we're detained here Professor Rowland and I have once again been able to generate the

TAG field and we believe we can return the moon to its original orbit. However, we need three rare-earth elements to make it strong enough to work at the greater distance involved. Elizabeth has a list of the elements we need. Please give them to her and help her return here so we can complete our project. Once that is accomplished, we plan to escape using the Icarus wings. If all works as planned, I will see you both soon.

I love you both and miss you very much,
Vivien

Merlin had wiped the tears from his eyes and hugged Elizabeth. Tanner, stoic as ever, had said nothing, but his eyes were more glassy than usual. Merlin had taken the list from Elizabeth.

"Let's see. You need dysprosium, samarium and, what's this, yttrium? He was mumbling to himself. "I hope we have what you need." He had immediately rushed down to the storage facilities to search for the missing ingredients.

Now, holding the bag, she knew her mission, or at least this part of it, had succeeded. She wanted to leave tonight. It was late afternoon and the sun would soon be going down. She looked expectantly at Tanner.

As if knowing what she was thinking, he shook his head. "I know you want to leave right away. We need to plan this out and that will take time. All we have is this evening and tomorrow if you want to leave by tomorrow night. That still isn't much time, but I understand it's important you get back."

"Very important. I don't know how they've managed to keep my disappearance a secret, or even if they have, I've been gone so long."

"Let's get some dinner and start making plans," said Tanner. "In case your plans of escape are thwarted, you will have our help as backup."

"I have to agree with Tanner," said Merlin. "In fact…"

"You can agree all you want," interrupted Tanner, "but you're staying here. Don't even think about going Merlin."

"How did you know…? Never mind. I know I'll never win that battle."

"Sorry Merlin." Tanner squeezed his shoulder. "I know you want to see Grandma. So do I, but I really need you here."

"Okay. And I know you're being kind, but you think I'm getting too old for dangerous adventure." Tanner just shrugged.

"I'm starved," said Elizabeth. "Let's go eat."

Later that evening, Elizabeth sat on her bed, too wound up to sleep. Earlier, they had discussed different strategies. She had disclosed the plans put together with Vivien and her father and how they intended to escape once the moon was back in orbit. Yet, she couldn't help but consider all the other people Residuum was holding captive. Perhaps they could somehow go back later and free them.

Thoughts were swirling through her head. Soon, she would be back. If the TAG field worked, and the earth's moon was returned to its orbit and the climate stabilized,

183

then her dream would be actualized. She knew it was just the beginning and there was still much that could go wrong. The Shell brothers were not stupid. If she and the others were not extremely careful, their plans could be uncovered and their intent revealed.

Terrence was especially troublesome. Lately she had been bothered by the way he looked at her and the strange glint in his eyes. Then he would smile that smug smile of his as if he had a delicious secret that he had no intention of sharing. She shivered inwardly and tried to think about something else.

Terrence wandered around feeling irritated and restless. He needed to talk to Elizabeth. He felt she had been avoiding him recently and now she was in quarantine. Obviously, he couldn't go anywhere near her till she was out of there. He had plans for the two of them. He had finally decided to take a partner and she was his chosen one. She had spirit; he would enjoy breaking it. She would soon find out who was making the rules and who was obeying them. He smiled to himself just thinking about it.

When he reached his destination, he looked up to read the engraved sign above a wide door: The Brotherhood. He had decided to see his genesis brothers, as they always put him in a good mood. They were housed in the finest facilities in the place. They had access to instruction in all the sciences, an up-to-date gym, the best food, martial arts and weapons training. And best of all, they loved him and his brother unconditionally.

Taking out his keys, he unlocked the door. The door opened into a wide hallway. He could hear talking in the dining hall, so he headed that direction.

Entering the doorway, he smiled widely and yelled out, "Hello brothers." Sitting at long tables, twenty-four brothers ages fifteen to nineteen turned at once, smiling at him with fondness and love. Together they called out in unison, voices blending together, "Hello brother Terrence." He gazed at his brothers happily then swept across the floor with a flourish and settled in comfortably among them.

Chapter Thirty One

Elizabeth woke up with a start, frightened by a dream. As it slowly began to recede, she sat up and sipped on a glass of water, her hands trembling. In the dream she was trying to run from Terrence. She could barely move. He easily caught up to her and suddenly morphed into two people, then three, all laughing hideously. Soon she found herself surrounded by leering faces with darting eyes, all looking like Terrence. She called out to Tanner for help and the countless faces twisted into hate-filled rage, the gray eyes spewing out hot molten lead, melting and distorting the faces. Clawing hands reached out to choke her. She had awakened abruptly.

Now, soaked in sweat, she looked at the clock. It was five thirty in the morning. A shiver swept through her. The dream had seemed so real. It brought back one of her earliest memories of Terrence. Once when they were around ten years old they had been in the same study group for a while, before he quit going.

She remembered his eyes because they were never still, always darting here and there. It had bothered her and she had been uncomfortable looking at him. She was glad when he no longer showed up.

Sighing as the dream slowly receded and knowing she would never get back to sleep, she decided to get up. Wearily moving about the room, she heard a soft tap on the door. "Are you all right in there?" She heard Tanner's muffled voice on the other side of the door. Easing the door open, she gestured him in.

"I was walking by on my way to the dining hall when I heard you cry out," he said, looking at her disheveled state. "Are you all right?"

"Just a bad dream." She wrapped her arms around herself, pulling her long pajama shirt close around her, shivering.

Tanner noticed and without hesitation he put his arms around her and pulled her in close. "Everything will be fine. You don't have anything to worry about because I am going back with you."

"What?" Elizabeth pulled back and looked up. "We agreed you would arrive after we returned the moon to its correct orbital coordinates. You can't go back with me now. We have to insure the success of the project first."

"I am going back with you to make sure you get there safely. Once you're in safe hands, I'm going to walk back. From what I've gathered, it's on the north side, close to

187

the other entrance. I can make it back easily. The night stalkers are no threat anymore, as long as I have a bright flashlight. Besides, I want to see Grandma. You can't deny a guy the chance to see his grandmother who, I might remind you, he hasn't seen in twenty years?"

Elizabeth smiled and relaxed back into his arms. He had a way of disarming her. "No I suppose that would be very insensitive on my part now wouldn't it?"

"Yes, very insensitive," he whispered hoarsely. "It would just ruin your image." She looked up and at once became inescapably enveloped in the brown depths of his eyes. He bent his head down and kissed her. A sweet kiss, long enough to say something but too short to say it all, and it left her wanting more.

Tanner leaned back, pushing her unruly hair behind her ears, his face revealing nothing. "I'll meet you in the dining hall. We still have a lot of plans to go over."

"Yes, plans," was all Elizabeth managed to get out. Her brain suddenly didn't seem to be working very well. Where he was concerned, she kept running into walls of confusion. Tanner smiled, turned and walked out the door, closing it quietly behind him.

The air turned cold as Tanner's warmth left with him. Elizabeth shivered again, realizing for the first time that her feelings for Tanner went much deeper than she was willing to admit.

Tanner stood outside Elizabeth's door for a moment, collecting himself and wondering why he had, without any hesitation on his part, kissed her. He knew exactly why.

Those beautiful green eyes drew him in and he couldn't resist. That and she had looked so vulnerable and alone.

He slowly made his way to the dining hall. Feeling muddled and a little confused, he knew he couldn't let himself get distracted. Unexpectedly and in short order she had become a part of his life, and that hadn't happened before.

Sure, he'd been in relationships with women, short lived, and he had told them up front that it couldn't be more than physical. He had remained emotionally unavailable until now. With Elizabeth it was different. He actually felt something for her, and he didn't know if he liked the feeling.

He entered the dining hall and saw Merlin eating breakfast. After ordering some food from Gertie, he sat down across from Merlin. Merlin pushed his empty plate back and grabbed his coffee cup. "I'm getting a refill. I'll be right back."

Settling back down, Merlin sipped on his hot coffee. Setting his cup down, he pulled a small device out of his pocket and laid it on the table. "Will came up with a handy communication device. He found the satellite wave band Residuum is using. After much trial and error, he found another frequency they won't pick up. Elizabeth can use that frequency to communicate to us when she goes back. According to Elizabeth, Residuum has satellite towers on top of the mountain and they are still in service."

Tanner turned the device over in his hand, studying it. "You mean they are still using satellites orbiting the earth?"

"Yes, they were not all destroyed, only the ones that were in the anti-gravity field. That is how they are able to use GPS to keep track of all their people."

"Wow. That is unbelievable." Tanner handed the device back.

"Yes it is, and we can use it to our advantage. Elizabeth can communicate to us as to when they will be generating the field. It's only one-way, though. We can't risk communicating back."

Elizabeth walked up to the table, having heard the last of Merlin's conversation. "Also, you will know if it works because that bright star up there will be dropping toward the earth pretty fast. When it gets closer, to anyone observing the night sky, it will obviously be the moon. There are going to be some scared people out there when they see the moon plunging to the earth. It's going to look like it's heading on a collision course straight for us. In fact, if we don't shut the field off when the moon gets into its correct orbital distance from the earth, the earth and moon will collide."

"And that would be a major catastrophe."

"Yes, the earth could not withstand an impact of that magnitude," replied Elizabeth. "However, that's not going to happen. Once the anti-gravity field is off, the moon will immediately stabilize into its former orbit, well actually a little bit closer. The moon lost some of its mass when it was struck by the meteor, so we have changed the coordinates to reflect that missing mass."

Elizabeth picked up the device on the table. "So, I will be able to communicate with you?"

190

"Yes," Merlin nodded. "We discovered a frequency Residuum can't pick up."

"Keep in touch with us as to your progress. It's text only. When you're ready to escape," Tanner added, "we will be there to help."

Gertie brought Tanner's breakfast over and took Elizabeth's order. "Just toast and coffee please. I'm not very hungry." Stress always affected her appetite. Apparently Tanner didn't have that problem; he was wolfing down a huge plate filled with eggs and potatoes.

"We still have some minor things to iron out in our plans," Merlin said as he rose to go. "We can meet back here in two hours. I'm going to the cabin and check on Cara now. She's going back to the mutant camp to tell Doc she's okay. I have found a job for her here if that's okay with you Tanner. She would like to stay."

"If you think she's trustworthy and she has a job, that's fine with me," Tanner said between mouthfuls.

Merlin nodded and turned to go. "Oh, Elizabeth, I also have a note I want you to give to Vivien. I'll give it to you before you leave."

"Of course, Merlin." He left and she was alone again with Tanner, who was busy finishing off his plate of food. Gertie brought over her toast and she nibbled on it as she sipped her coffee.

Pushing back his empty plate, Tanner glanced at Elizabeth's plate of toast. "You really should eat more, you know. You will need your strength to get you through the coming days."

"I know. I'm just not hungry. I will eat more at lunch and dinner."

"Promise?'

"Yes, I promise."

"Good." He stood up to go. "I need to organize some things. I will meet you back here in a couple of hours."

Elizabeth nodded. After he left, she pushed her half eaten toast aside. Her insides were jittery. The dream had unsettled her. She hoped Terrence had not discovered her missing in the two weeks she had been gone. She had no idea what she was going back to and that thought terrified her.

Chapter Thirty Two

Terrence was literally with his brothers. Sure, they had been taken from his father's frozen sperm and placed in the wombs of the most intelligent women on the earth. But they were biologically his brothers, even though some had lighter brown hair and there were a few without the gray eyes, the resemblance was still startling.

It was too bad for the women they hadn't been able to share in the success of the brotherhood but, unfortunately, they had been comatose. It was the only option. His father had known that women of that intelligence were not going to willingly spend the rest of their lives having his babies, so he really had no choice. Spencer had tried to reason with them, but to no avail.

Spencer had only one need for their intelligence: to use for the future generations. He came up with the brilliant plan of using the one thing they had that he needed, their wombs and their eggs. He would impregnate them with his sperm, only bringing male fetuses to term. He had five women delivering five sons a year with three months used to replenish their systems. Special nurseries were set up to care for them. Spencer's dream had been for a new superior race, seeded by him, to evolve into superior beings. They would be the elite of Residuum.

Everything had gone according to plan for two years. Only one child had died at birth. Unfortunately, during the third year, when the women had just been impregnated, there had been a power outage that had lasted for a week. The women were unable to survive without medical assistance.

Other women were used to bare the female babies and the generic male babies. These women wore a little luckier; they were aware of their condition. The birthing women were not too happy about it, especially the ones who were incubating four or five babies at once, but they had

193

ways of keeping them in line. After all, it was for the good of Residuum and the future of the earth; the earth needed to be repopulated, having lost millions upon millions of people during and after the holocaust.

He looked around him and smiled. His nine brothers were eighteen to nineteen years of age, strong, intelligent and fit. A month after birth they were fitted with neural implants similar to the ones he and Winston had. The implants made his genesis brothers more intelligent with the added benefit of a program written into the implant that dictated their loyalty to Residuum and the original sons of Shell.

It was perfect. He basked in his brothers' love and affection. They would do anything for him including die for him. Wasn't life wonderful? Brandishing a glass of juice, he held it up in a toast to the brotherhood of Residuum. His brothers jostled to get close to him. Terrence was feeling much better.

Winston leaned back in his chair, a smile on his face. Everything was going according to plan. Soon Residuum would have control of the whole eastern Rocky Mountain chain from southern Colorado to Wyoming. The Manitou colony didn't stand a chance and in short order his forces would hit Academy and Pueblo.

There was nothing happening in Denver. It was a wasteland. The small bands of people along the river were no threat. The only threat was in southern Wyoming. Laramie had survived much of the destruction and the university there had created an effective bomb shelter beforehand, and many had survived through the worst of it. They had subsequently developed a thriving community and were reaching out to other settlements to form some kind of united front.

Winston laughed out loud. He would soon put a stop to that. After he secured the local area, he would turn his attention to Laramie. Right now, he was more concerned with Terrence. Frowning, he considered his brother. Why, at times, was Terrence inexplicably hot headed and emotionally agitated. The implant should have reversed that tendency. He was better after he spent time in the brotherhood, but Terrence should be in control at all times. Should he be worried? For Winston, losing command of one's emotions was unthinkable. Winston equated intelligence with control, so he was apprehensive with his brother's lack of it.

They were too close to realizing their dreams of conquest and subjugation. His army understood what it meant to be well fed and clothed and considering they didn't like the inevitable screeching in their ear when they disobeyed, they would fight for him, His elite brotherhood would oversee his acquisitions. After all, it was for humanities own good. In order to return to some semblance of order in the world of today, there must be a supreme ruler and that supreme ruler must exercise authority with an iron fist.

Tidying a stack of papers on his desk, Winston's lightening-speed thoughts raced ahead to the future. Once the hierarchy becomes established, he reasoned, everyone will have their place. He laughed quietly to himself knowing, with his heightened perception, that the ability to utilize his enhanced intelligence and rationale would insure ultimate victory. As a result of that, order would be restored once again.

He knew with their technology and weapons, the small army in his control, night stalkers to elicit fear, and the wings for surveillance, they would be unstoppable. Of course, the only dilemma he now faced was Lane and Rowland's inability to complete the wave field. Unfortunately, he needed them.

Without the moon back in its former orbit, there would be no future. Once they accomplished that, he could do away with them. Elizabeth was another matter. Terrence had announced recently, he would take her for his mate. Maybe that would calm him down. Winston certainly hoped so.

*   *   *

Elizabeth was nervous. They had finished discussing the final plans earlier that morning and Merlin suggested she rest till evening. She still had no appetite, but knew she needed to eat a substantial lunch and dinner. She went back to the dining hall to have lunch, thinking about the upcoming flight back to Cheyenne Mountain. It was a small comfort that Tanner would be accompanying her, but it also created stress and worry. What if something happened to him? Elizabeth couldn't live with that.

They would leave right after sunset. She was thankful for the homing device on the wings because it would take them right to the opening in the mountain.

However, they must get there in that half hour window when it would be open.

Entering the dining hall, she saw Merlin eating lunch at the counter. Joining him, he turned and smiled. "Good to see you back here," he said. "Order something filling."

Elizabeth smiled back and said to Gertie, "Give me a large sub sandwich with the works."

"That's my girl," Merlin patted her hand. "Everything is going to work out. We will take them by surprise. Residuum won't know what hit them."

"I hope you're right Merlin," Elizabeth sighed. She admired Merlin's confidence, but she knew the ruthlessness of the Shell brothers and she wondered if she was sending her friends on a suicide mission. Did they really know what they were up against?

Chapter Thirty Three

Cara was close to the mutant camp, having left early in the morning after eating a hearty breakfast. Merlin had insisted she eat it. She hadn't argued. He had given her some dried food to take along and she had it in her pack with some water. So far it had been an uneventful journey. She had seen some rovers out, but they had ignored her, hurrying off on some important mission.

She could see the smoke from the campfires and stoves. It was almost noon, so she had made good time. She would have to cross the river, but that would be easy as there was a makeshift bridge beside the camp. As she crossed, she noticed the river had gone down considerably from the last time she had been here. She didn't understand why the weather had changed and it had become warm year-round, but she knew it had something to do with the moon.

She saw a small figure running from the first small rows of cabins. She recognized little Ernie. He waved with his one arm and called out her name. She bent down when he neared and scooped him up in a warm hug.

"You're back," he called out cheerfully. "Doc was getting worried about you. Not me, though. I knew you could take care of yourself."

"Is that so?" Carrie replied. She carefully sat him back down. Like so many of the mutants he had physical disabilities, but he didn't let it get him down. She gazed at his impish face, one bright eye sparkling in the sunlight, the other one missing. His lower right arm had been so deformed when he was born that Doc amputated it at the elbow.

Ernie had been left at the camp when he was only a few weeks old, snuggly wrapped in a homemade quilt, unwanted but alive. He grabbed her hand and walked with her to the middle of the encampment. She saw Doc outside talking to one of his aides. Groups of children were working or playing.

Doc greeted her as she approached. "I'm glad you're back. We were afraid the night stalkers had taken you."

"No," Cara lied. "I decided to go to Manitou and see if they needed any help at their settlement."

"Oh? How's Merlin?"

"He's fine. He wanted me to give you his greetings and asked if you needed anything? I'm heading back tomorrow and I can give him a message. He says I can stay there as long as I work."

"Well, you know you are always welcome here, but I understand if you need a change of pace. It's hard work here, but it's finally paying off. The mutations have all but stopped. Women are baring healthy babies and are happy to keep them, so we have more room. The older ones are now teaching the young children and we've enough shelter for everyone."

"Aren't you worried about the rising water? I've been told it's getting nearer."

"Well, we'll worry about that when the time comes. We've lived through an unimaginable destruction and aftermath and I'm not giving up now." Cara smiled and nodded her head in agreement.

"When you return to Manitou, tell Merlin we need a few medical supplies. I'll give you a list before you go."

"Okay. I'm going to my cabin to rest." Cara said goodbye to Ernie and hurried back toward the river to a cabin at the end of the first row. She rushed to the door, excitement bubbling over. Opening the door, she glanced around, her chest tightening. There was no one in the little cabin. Disappointment washed over her. He's not here. She slumped down on the mattress in the corner, feeling defeated.

She didn't know how long she sat there. She needed to get up and clean the place before she left in the morning, but couldn't seem to move. Her plans didn't mean much to her anymore, not now. Unable to move, she stared blankly at the walls.

The door to her cabin opened abruptly. Cara looked up expectantly then jumped up, her heart in her throat. "You're still here!"

"Of course, I'm still here. Where else would I be?" Dwight McGee barreled into the room. "It's about time you got back. Doc has been putting me to work. He said if I didn't work, he was kicking me out. We need to get out of here."

Cara knew Dwight was a little rough around the edges, but she didn't care. She was so much in love with him it hurt. She jumped up and ran to him, throwing her arms around his neck. He gave her a quick hug and pulled away, trying to distance himself a little. She hung on, not wanting to let him go yet.

"What happened to you? Did you find anything out at Manitou?" he asked as he disentangled himself from her arms and shut the door.

"You will never believe what I found out," she teased as she sat in one of the chairs in the corner of the room.

"I don't have time for games," McGee answered, visibly irritated. He sat in the chair next to her. "Well?"

Cara licked her lips, brimming with important information, and she thrilled at being the center of his attention for as long as possible. "First of all, I was taken by night stalkers. They took me somewhere. I'm not sure where because I was unconscious. When I woke up I was at the Manitou settlement. It seems Tanner and a couple of his men saved me. Merlin said I could come back and they would have a job for me."

"Inside?" McGee asked, his eyes widening with excitement.

"Yes, inside." Cara answered with satisfaction.

"Yes!" McGee stood up and raised his arms in fists, looking up at the ceiling in something near ecstasy.

"I'm going back with you," he finally said as he lowered his arms, glancing at Cara.

"Oh, I haven't told you everything." Cara drew in a deep breath, savoring the moment. "I heard Tanner say there's people in Cheyenne Mountain. He's going to be heading there soon. Something is going on."

"Even better," McGee grinned. "Who knows the treasures I'll find in that mountain. I've heard the rumors about the people in there and how they have riches beyond anything we have out here." He began pacing, making plans in his head. He was also going to take out Tanner. Nobody embarrasses him without paying for it.

"We're leaving tomorrow," he stated abruptly. "I'll stay in old Manitou Springs while you go back to their settlement and get more information. When you find out when they're leaving, you'll get in touch with me immediately and I'll be right behind them." He smiled down at her. "You did good Cara."

"What's my reward?" She purred.

McGee roughly pulled her out of the chair. He grabbed her hair and pulled her head back. Her eyes filled with lust. "I know how you like it," he snarled. "When I'm done with you, you'll be hurting all over."

McGee grabbed her around the waist and threw her on the mattress. She landed hard on her stomach and quickly turned over, spreading herself out on the bed in anticipation. She moaned with pleasure as he leapt on top of her.

Chapter Thirty Four

As evening approached, Elizabeth remained filled with apprehension. So much could go wrong. She spread the wings out on her bed. Silver feathers glittered in the lamplight. She took a deep breath to give her strength. There was a soft rap on the door. Opening it, she found Merlin standing in the corridor, looking a little lost. He held a letter in his hand.

"This is for Vivien." He handed it to her. "Tell her… tell her…" He looked away, wiping at his eyes."

"I know Merlin." Elizabeth put it in her pocket and lifted the wings gently. It's time to go isn't it?" He nodded. "Why do I feel like I'm about to leap into an unknown abyss?"

"In many ways you are." Merlin cleared his throat, as he followed her into the hallway, closing the door behind him. "You've been gone far too long. You just realized who you are and you probably feel like you're taking a desperate gamble. Not only do you have to successfully complete your project, but you have to get out safely."

Elizabeth and Merlin walked side by side down the corridor. They were meeting Tanner at the back entrance and then they'd be off. He had the pack full of the necessary rare elements to complete the battery created for the wave field.

As they rounded the corner, she saw Tanner up ahead, leaning against the side of the corridor, talking to Joe. When he saw them, he levered himself away from the wall. Any misgivings he had were hidden, his face a mask. Elizabeth squared her shoulders and straightened her spine, trying to ease her fear.

"Take care of Elizabeth, Tanner, and make sure she gets there safely," Merlin instructed, as they drew near.

"That's the plan." Tanner assured him. Elizabeth gave Merlin a quick hug. Tanner picked up the pack and Elizabeth held on to the wings as they hurried out the door.

Tanner called out over his shoulder as they stepped through the doorway. "I'll be back soon. It should be before daybreak." Merlin nodded, his eyes filled with a combination of uncertainty and hope. The door closed behind them. Outside, the wind hushed through the trees and the final rays of sunset painted the trunks in shadows of black and silver.

"It will be very dark soon," Tanner muttered. Elizabeth opened the wings and turned on the homing device. Tanner harnessed them in, strapping the backpack to the front of Elizabeth. He nodded across the purple night sky and they rose into the air, heading toward Cheyenne Mountain.

Flying over the dark canopy of trees, the cool wind caressed Elizabeth's face, soothing her chaotic mind. Above them, the stars sparkled in their brilliance; below them the darkness was nearly impenetrable. They glided in that in-between space, not belonging wholly to either world, yet a small part of both.

Without the homing device they would have missed it. The portal on the side of a cliff blended in with the deep darkness of the night. It was still closed; they were early. Hovering over it, Elizabeth pointed to a small ledge they could perch on until hopefully, it would open. They were soon precariously balanced on the side of a cliff that would have been impossible to get to without the wings.

"How much longer till nine o clock?" Elizabeth asked.

"We have about ten minutes," Tanner replied, his arms holding her close, as if he was afraid Elizabeth might fall. "I'll keep the power on in case I slip. I wouldn't want us to tumble off this cliff." He glanced down into blackness, unable to see the treetops below.

Elizabeth said a prayer, not really knowing to whom. She just put it out there, onto the earth and hoped some higher power was listening. It was a prayer for the safety of her friends and loved ones. Her mind becoming tangential, she asked herself in which category would she put Tanner? She glanced up at him; he was looking to the west, his expression one of hopeful wonder. She knew he was looking at the far away moon.

She grabbed his hand, smiled and nodded. Without warning, the portal opened. They were ready. As Elizabeth looked below to make sure it was safe, Tanner raised his hand to press the lever to descend into the portal.

"Wait!" Elizabeth whispered frantically into his ear. She grabbed his arm and they stared wide-eyed, barely breathing, at the scene unfolding below them.

Professor Rowland and Vivien looked up when the portal opened. This was it, the last night. If Elizabeth didn't show up, they would have some difficult explaining to do. If the Shells decided to get the rare elements from the Manitou settlement, they would not ask nicely. Thinking about them seemed to suddenly evoke their presence. The two brothers

205

unexpectedly walked through the door as if they owned the place. In reality they did.

"Good evening, professor, doctor," Winston smoothly intoned. "We decided to pay you a visit this evening."

"What a pleasant surprise," lied Vivien, although she hoped she sounded somewhat believable.

"Maybe not so pleasant," smirked Terrence. "We are taking all the wings. We're going to put them in a more secure location. We wouldn't want anyone to disappear into the night now would we?" He looked up. "Why is the portal open?"

"We were testing the wave function," the professor replied. "We need it open for the best results."

"Is it complete? Winston asked.

"We have one last element to add," answered Vivien. "We should be ready within two weeks." More lies.

"Two weeks!" exclaimed Terrence, in a fury. "I want it ready now, do you hear me? Now!" He stepped forward with a hint of menace. Winston grabbed his arm, his lips set in a thin line, his expression dark.

"Terrence," he spoke softly into his ear. "We must be calm at all times." Terrence's black gaze hardened on Vivien and Albert. Sneering, he lunged past them, veering toward the storage room. Unlocking it, he banged the door open and hastily began grabbing the wings, carelessly throwing them into a cart.

"It is your optimistic expectation to have the project completed within two weeks, then?" Winston's question hung in the air. Though smiling, his hard gaze penetrated

206

them to their bones. Vivien cringed inwardly, feeling like he could read her mind. Mute, they both just nodded.

"Very well, keep us informed of your progress." He shot them one last hard-edged look before walking into the storage room. Wings haphazardly filled the cart as Terrence began pushing it out the door.

"I want to see Elizabeth in my office, first thing in the morning." Terrence's voice rang like a slap through the room. Albert and Vivien looked at the cart as he passed and nodded. Winston observed their looks of longing before they quickly covered them up. Was it possible they were planning to use them to flee? Why would they want to leave this safe haven he had provided for them? How absurd; no it couldn't be. It wouldn't matter anyway in the end.

Winston followed his brother out of the lab and down the corridor. The rumble of the cart grew distant, then silent. The room went hollow, all life sucked out of it.

Vivien slumped in defeat. "That was our only way out of here. So many people trusted us to help them out of this hellhole. It's hopeless." She wearily dropped into a chair, elbows on her knees and head in her hands.

The professor sat dejectedly beside her. He had no words of comfort for Vivien. Forever the optimist, he had perhaps given up too. They sat in the stillness of the lab, silent as the grave until a small rock fell at their feet. They looked at each other in surprise and looked up. Maybe? Only blackness filled the portal. Vivien looked at him, her own heartache and sorrow reflected in his face. She shook her head in sadness. They both knew they had reached the end of their endurance.

207

Another rock fell, then some pebbles. They both looked blankly at the floor, then up at the portal. They watched in shocked silence as silver wings dropped down from the portal and swooshed drunkenly to land directly in front of them. In disbelief they realized it was Elizabeth attached to the wings, or rather attached to a dark-haired, nice-looking young man who was attached to the wings.

Too stunned to move, they just sat there. As if suddenly awakened from a deep sleep, they both bolted to their feet. "Elizabeth, you're back!" Vivien cried. "Oh thank God, you're back." Elizabeth smiled as she unclasped the harness. The man with her just stared, his face hard.

"Who is this?" she asked in surprise. The man slowly smiled at her. She knew that smile. Her breath caught in the back of her throat, her heart leapt.

"Tanner? No… Oh, my God, it is… it is you." Tears began rolling freely down her face, as she stood frozen, not believing her eyes. Elizabeth broke free and ran to hug her father.

Tanner opened his arms wide. "Grandma." Still too dazed to move, Vivien took a deep breath and rubbed her eyes. Finally convinced he was real, she stumbled over to him, blinded by her tears. Tanner scooped her up; she hugged him tightly.

"It really is you. It's been so long. I have so much to tell you, so many questions to ask," she cried through her tears. Tanner pulled back, grinning while holding on to her shoulders. She wiped at her eyes, clearly overwhelmed. "Merlin… is he…?"

"Merlin is fine; ornery as ever." Vivien laughed and cried. "He sent a message with Elizabeth. Uh, Grandma, is there a safer place we can talk?" Tanner began to unfasten the harness to the wings. "I don't want those two jerks to walk in on this scene."

"Yes, yes, let's go into the storage facility. If we hear them coming back, there are many places to hide in there."

Regaining her senses, she turned toward the professor. "Albert, I want you to meet my grandson, Tanner. Tanner this is Professor Rowland, Elizabeth's father."

"Call me Albert," the professor shook Tanner's hand. Elizabeth hugged Vivien. They stepped into the storage facility and pushed the door almost closed.

"We've been so worried," Vivien began. "This was the last night before…"

"We know," Elizabeth interrupted. "We heard everything. We were just getting ready to fly down when the Shells arrived. It was this close." She held up her thumb and finger and pushed them together for emphasis.

"So you know. They took the wings. We just configured five more. We had a total of fifteen. Now they're gone. That was our way out and it's not just us. Many people want out of here. We were going to load as many people as we could on each set of wings. Come back for more if we have to. Now, we only have two. We can still do it. It will just take longer."

"You have two?" Elizabeth asked. "I thought this was the only one the Shells didn't know about."

"No, Stan delivered another one last week." Eyeing Elizabeth's pack, Vivien asked cautiously, "Were you able to obtain the elements we need?" Elizabeth nodded.

Vivien sagged with relief. "We should be able to actually get it done in the two weeks I told them, possibly sooner. I was lying to them earlier, stalling for time. Now it's actually conceivable."

"Grandma, you're not alone." Tanner assured her. "We are going to help you escape. Had we known about this place, we would have been here sooner. Because of Elizabeth, we found you."

"What took you so long, Elizabeth?" Albert asked.

"It's a long story Pop. To sum it up, I hit my head and lost my memory for a week and a half. When I regained it, I realized I had to get back here quickly. Tanner insisted on coming with me." She smiled at him.

"He is going to walk back, once I drop him off outside. Also, we can communicate with them. It's one-way. We can tell them when the project is complete and that we're ready to go. They will help us to get out."

"You're not walking back, Tanner," Vivien interjected. "You're taking the other pair of wings and flying back."

"You may need them, Grandma."

"I insist. Albert?" He nodded. "Besides, it'll be easier to get back. No arguing."

Tanner saluted. "If I remember right, I don't think I ever won an argument with you." Vivien's eyes filled with tears again. Elizabeth walked over and hugged her. She pushed the envelope from Merlin into her hand. Vivien

210

gazed at it, then put it in the pocket of her jacket. She would read it later when she was alone.

"I need to tell you about our plans before I leave," indicated Tanner. "There are many of us at the settlement who are willing to help. If everything goes right, we won't need all the wings."

"I want to hear everything about the success of the shelter Merlin built and what has happened out there."

"We have been very successful in the last twenty years," Tanner replied. "The people in the settlement are strong and they are happy. Merlin and I will tell you all about it, when we see you again."

Elizabeth nodded. "I will fill you in on everything I saw in the short time I was there."

"Thank you, Elizabeth."

"Now, we have to discuss our plans before I leave," Tanner leaned his fists on the edge of a table.

They gathered around and Vivien began explaining what they had spent so long plotting. Tanner listened intently; incredulous at the plan they had concocted and wondering how it could possibly work. After much haggling about tactics and strategies, he was eventually satisfied they could coordinate the time and events. The timing had to be perfect if they were to escape Cheyenne Mountain.

Chapter Thirty Five

They approached old Manitou Springs the following morning. When Cara and McGee had left the mutant camp earlier, the air had been cool and crisp. Now, four hours later, they were sweating from the heat. McGee held up his hand when they reached a split in the trail.

Armed with two rifles, several guns, ammunition, and knives, he was loaded down with weaponry of one sort or another. Still smarting from his roust when he attacked the settlement, this time, McGee vowed, it would be different. He would use stealth and of course Cara as his informant.

He'd heard there might be people in the area around the old deserted town. There were a few houses that hadn't been swept away in the floods and he wanted to make certain no one knew he was in the area.

Wiping the sweat from his brow, McGee pointed to a trail that angled off to the south. "That's the trail to the settlement. I'll be in one of the houses farther up the main trail here." He nodded to the west. "When you have information, go up there and find me. Got it?"

Cara nodded. She stepped over to him and hugged him goodbye. He patted her quickly then held her back by the shoulders, looking squarely into her eyes. "Remember, I need to know when they are heading to Cheyenne Mountain. I can't hang out around the settlement because those wolves will start howling and warn them. They also have lookouts.

You're safe and can come and go. It's less than an hour to their settlement, so once you find out anything get over here and let me know. Okay?"

"What if it takes a while to find out anything?" Cara asked.

"Report every two or three days. Bring me some food. I know they have plenty there." Cara nodded and turned to go. McGee slapped her hard on her backside. "I'm counting on you. Don't let me down."

"I won't. I'll be back in two days."

"That's my girl," McGee grinned.

They parted ways. Cara waved one last time before she lost sight of him through the trees. Once they got the treasures from Cheyenne Mountain, they would be together. Dwight was the love of her life and she knew she could make him love her. It was just a matter of time. And now that she was helping him, he would appreciate her even more.

Cara knew Doc hadn't approved of her leaving with him. She didn't care. She smiled to herself, knowing she had Dwight right where she wanted him. Once she proved to him how much she could help him, he would never let her go. They had a bond. That thought buoyed her spirits and, though tired, she picked up her pace.

"Stupid bitch," McGee mumbled under his breath as he drew farther away from Cara.

McGee cautiously made his way toward the few standing houses. He spied smoke coming out of the chimney of a well-kept cabin. Hiding behind a large rock, he grimaced as he sat down to wait. Though burning with impatience, he needed to know just how many people were living up here.

Cara was nearing the cabin. She knew the wolves were close by; she sensed their presence with a snap of a twig, a low growl. Although Merlin said her clothes had been initiated and the wolves would not harm her, she still worried. She felt relief when she spotted the cabin through the woods and heard Raini's greeting from above.

"Hello, Raini," she answered back, waving a hand in the general direction of Raini's voice. "I'm glad to be back. Is Merlin around?"

"He was just out front. I think he's puttering around in the cabin." Right then Merlin stepped out the front door and raised his hand in greeting as she came out of the woods.

"How was your trip?" he asked when she drew near.

"Fine. No one bothered me." Cara reached in her pocket. "Here's a list from Doc. He sends his best wishes and says there's no hurry."

Merlin glanced down at the list before nodding and stuffing it in his pocket. "I've talked to Tanner and he says you can room in the dorm inside the cave. Right now, we need help in the garden. We have many plants and herbs to harvest and prepare for food and medicine."

"That's fine with me. I don't mind hard work."

"Okay. I'll show you your room and give you a tour of the gardens." Cara nodded and smiled gleefully to herself as she followed Merlin into the cabin and through the door into the settlement.

After enjoying a stew he had made, Ben stepped outside the door intent on getting some wood from behind

215

the cabin. He had been on the lookout yesterday for any trespassers but things were quiet as usual. Not many people came out this far as it was out of the way from the main trail. Looking around, he nodded to himself and walked around to the back of the cabin.

On his way back, arms loaded, he thought he heard a sound. He glanced over his shoulder. Seeing nothing, he again made his way toward the door. A gunshot blast split the air. Ben lurched forward, wood flying in all directions, and fell heavily to the ground. Blood oozed out of the gunshot wound and spread across his back.

McGee lowered the rifle and stepped around the rock. He approached the old man's lifeless body. He leaned over it, seeing the blank stare. Straightening up, McGee looked around him in satisfaction. Earlier, his patience had nearly run out. As far as he could tell, there was one old man in the cabin. The other houses appeared to be empty and he had realized earlier that there was a good chance no one else lived up here.

"Well, it looks like I got a place to live for a while." He sniffed the air. "Sure smells good in there. Thanks for lunch old man." He sidestepped the body. He would take care of it after he'd had a bite to eat." Ambling toward the door, he chuckled to himself and stepped inside the cabin.

Chapter Thirty Six

Tanner slept late. Returning in the early morning hours, after extensive planning with the professor, his grandmother, and Elizabeth, he had hid the wings in his closet and passed out on his bed from sheer exhaustion. Now, enjoying a late breakfast in the dining hall, he looked up to see Merlin enter followed by the woman he had saved in Cheyenne Mountain.

Merlin approached. "Tanner, I want to introduce you to Cara. She will be working in the gardens." He nodded, sipping his coffee.

"Glad to meet you," Cara nodded back. "Thank you for getting me away from the night stalkers."

"No problem. We help when we can," he acknowledged.

"I was out of it at the time. Where exactly did you find me?" Cara asked.

Tanner glanced at Merlin. "In a cave not too far from here," he answered.

"Do you see many in the area?"

"Not really." Changing the topic Tanner inquired, "So, you'll be helping in the gardens, huh? We appreciate your help. Thank you." There was finality to his tone, as he stood to go. Cara doubted conversational inquiry would get her anywhere, or at least not get her the answers she wanted. She needed to shift their interaction to a different plane.

Smiling suggestively at Tanner, she looked him up and down saying, "I look forward to getting to know you." Tanner glanced at Cara, expressionless, nodded, then turned to take his empty dishes to the counter.

"I'll introduce you to Gertie and the kitchen help," Merlin said cheerily. "Then we'll get a bite to eat. Are you hungry?" Merlin headed for the counter, Cara following.

Replying in a low husky voice, as she caught Tanner's eye, "I'm very hungry." She brushed his shoulder as he walked by her on his way out.

Stepping into the corridor, Tanner thought that was certainly awkward. He knew a flirt when he saw one. There was a time when he just might have taken her up on what she was offering. She was attractive enough, though a little rough around the edges. He kept seeing emerald eyes in a beautiful face surrounded by auburn hair, eyes that mesmerized him with their depth.

He drew in a tight breath. He had work to do. It didn't include daydreaming about Elizabeth. Although, she had returned safely, he was still worried about her. Anything could go wrong. He only hoped her meeting today with that loony Terrence didn't put her in any danger. From what he had seen the night before, Tanner didn't trust Terrence's psychological state of mind. Thinking of Elizabeth alone with him left him in a state of extreme unease and he didn't like it.

Halting outside the door to Terrence's office, Elizabeth hesitated. Uncertainty and foreboding engulfed her. She didn't really know Terrence that well and had never felt comfortable around him. After Spencer died, Terrence had changed, and she barely recognized the smug, condescending tyrant he had become.

219

She drew in a deep breath and quietly knocked. An irritated voice from inside ordered her to enter. She opened the door and stepped inside the room. Feeling uncomfortable, she left the door open behind her.

Terrence was sitting alone at his desk, immersed in paperwork. Not looking up, he said, "Close the door behind you." Elizabeth did as he requested. Still absorbed in his work, he gestured to the chair in front of his desk. Closing the door, she sat down, hands in her lap. He continued working for several more minutes, then finally closed his notebook and looked up.

Greeting him with a quiet good morning, she glanced at him, briefly searching his eyes. He seemed normal enough. His eyes were focused on her; they didn't waver. She remembered the dream and his eyes. Suddenly chilled, she looked away, studying the picture on the wall. She hoped she had not betrayed her unease in his presence.

He studied her for a moment, as if debating what to say. Then he inquired about her health. Knowing his fear of contamination, she assured him she was fine.

Terrence could sense her unease. It gave him a feeling of power. He had always felt inferior to her, even with the computer chip that increased his ability to comprehend and remember. She took her intellect for granted, something he would never do. Well, now he had the upper hand.

After several long minutes, Terrence stirred. Leaning toward her he said, "You are probably wandering why I wanted you to come to my office this morning."

""Yes, I am," she replied, raising her eyebrows in question. "We work in different areas of the complex, so we rarely have work-related problems to consider."

"I don't just work in this complex." His voice sounded strained. "My brother and I are the president and vice-president of Residuum. We make the laws here." He leaned back gazing at her as if to gage her reaction. Elizabeth said nothing.

"A new law went into effect while you were in the decontamination unit," Terrence continued. "It concerns our highest priority, the future generation of children for Residuum. We will soon be expanding outward and we need a guarantee that our people will multiply and still remain faithful to this establishment. We will soon govern this whole area."

Elizabeth nodded, still not comprehending what this had to do with her.

"In order to do that, men must take wives and raise families that bow to the new government. A man is now allowed to choose his wife. It is his choice, not hers. He will be head of the family and his wife and children will obey him and his decisions." His face had set, the lines harsh and unyielding, his eyes dark.

Elizabeth sat frozen, unable to move, unable to draw a breath. She realized with dread where this was leading. Keeping her features bland, she nodded noncommittally.

His eyes softened a little as he studied her, thinking, assessing. "So, lucky for you I have made my choice. You will be my wife."

She bowed her head, seemingly in deference to the news, when actually she was trying to hide her revulsion and shock. She knew she had to play along and she hoped he hadn't arranged the marriage for today. She suppressed a shiver.

Raising her head, she smiled. "I am honored, but pardon my surprise. You gave me quite a shock. I need time, time to get used to the idea. We need to get to know one another again. We have rarely seen each other in the last few years."

"We'll have plenty of time to get to know one another." His gaze shifted to her body and back to her face. "We will at once begin to create a family. After all, that's the main purpose of our marriage."

Elizabeth's throat was dry as sand paper. She tried to swallow. "When…when is the marriage to take place? The field is nearly ready and I must focus on that. Can we wait until the project is complete? In fact we hope to be ready by the end of the week as everything has fallen into place sooner than expected." If he only knew, she thought. She smiled sweetly, hoping she hid her dismay over the unhappy prospect of marrying him.

Terrence frowned. He had not expected this reaction. He'd thought she would have flatly refused and walked out. She seemed to have lost her spunk. He had wanted to force her. Make her marry him and then crush her spirit. He hadn't expected her to be so agreeable. This wasn't any fun.

He thought quickly. He could still bend her to his will. He needed time anyway, time to… He grinned knowingly. He had a great idea. "Okay, we will wait until the project is complete. On that night, when the moon has been successfully returned to its orbit, we will marry. What better sign of success than that, don't you agree?"

Elizabeth nodded. She had to get out of there. The air was stifling and she couldn't breathe.

"Will that be all?" She asked with a smile.

"Not quite." Terrence rose from his chair, walked around his desk and approached the back of her chair. He grasped her shoulders and awkwardly began to rub them. Elizabeth froze. Moving his hands to the back of her neck, he caressed the area before slowly wrapping them around her neck and squeezing, not forcibly but enough for Elizabeth to feel the pressure.

Leaning his head down, she felt his breath against her cheek as he whispered into her ear, "You are mine Elizabeth."

Chapter Thirty Seven

Elizabeth stood for a moment outside the door. Emotion burned in her chest and she struggled to control it. Now that a door was between them, panic engulfed her. She was shaking, shuddering in every part of her body. Taking a deep breath, she tried to blot out his last threatening words. She couldn't.

After his dire declaration, he had slowly removed his hands from her neck and calmly taken his seat behind the desk. "That will be all," he had said, not even looking in her direction.

She had longed to bolt for the door. Instead, she had gradually risen and calmly walked to the door, quietly opening it and closing it behind her.

Trying to subdue her anxiety, she started slowly down the corridor, heading toward the lab. She didn't want to tell her father or Vivien. They already had too much to worry about. For now, she would keep it to herself. After all, she reasoned, their marriage would never happen anyway.

By the time she stepped into the lab, she felt more in control of her emotions. Vivien looked up from her work and smiled as she entered. She studied Elizabeth for a moment before asking her if she was all right.

"I'm fine," she reassured her. "I just don't like being in the same room as Terrence."

"I know what you mean. What did he want anyway?"

"Oh, just an update on our work. I assured him things were going well and that we were even ahead of schedule. That seemed to brighten his mood."

"Well, that's good. We don't like a moody Terrence." Vivien laughed dryly. "Anyway, we are ahead of schedule. Within a week we will begin the final stages of project moonshine. Once we process the remaining elements, we can begin generating the field."

Elizabeth was overjoyed. She would not let her experience with Terrence ruin her day. She had work to do. Sitting down beside Vivien, they were soon absorbed in the project details.

The door opened. Terrence looked up smugly, expecting Elizabeth to have come back begging for her freedom. "Oh, it's you." He resumed his work.

"Greetings brother. I'm glad to see you, too."

"Sorry Winston," he replied, glancing up at his brother. "Unfortunately, I'm rather busy at the moment. I'm preparing our army for the assault on Manitou. It is the strongest settlement in the area; therefore, it will need to go first. The rest will fall like dominoes."

"The night stalkers are ready," Winston said as he sat in the chair in front of the desk. "The army will kill all the men and capture the women. The night stalkers will back them up after dark, apprehending any women that might have escaped and herd them back to our facility. The men will then have their pick of the women."

Terrence glanced up. "The older brothers will get first pick. They get the best. Their seed will secure the intelligence of the future generations who will be the leaders of Residuum. I have already secured my choice. Elizabeth has agreed. She is honored that I would choose her."

Winston studied his brother. He knew Elizabeth. He didn't believe she would willingly accept the new conditions of marriage. Why would she so easily appease his brother? Something did not feel right. Of course his logic always outweighed his feelings, so he needed time to examine and evaluate this unwelcome emotional response.

"When will you wed?"

"Within the week. She said they are ahead of schedule. When the moon is once again in close orbit, we will wed, that very night. The next day, after a refreshing night of marital bliss, I will be ready for the upcoming battle. The Residuum forces will begin the takeover of this area." His eyes shined brightly with suppressed excitement as he gazed at Winston.

Winston nodded in approval. "We can be ready in a week. Everything is going as planned. I have a few things that need to be resolved, minor hindrances that can be easily managed."

Standing up to go, Winston smiled at Terrence. "Once the men know what the spoils of battle are, they will be much more agreeable to fighting for us." His laughter followed him out the door as Terrence chuckled to himself in amusement.

Chapter Thirty Eight

No word yet. Three days had passed and Tanner remained filled with a growing sense of unease. What if the communication device didn't work? Worse yet, what if it had been discovered by one of those loony brothers? Questions kept rolling through his mind, as he pushed his empty plate away and gulped down the last of his coffee.

His meeting earlier that morning had gone well. Tweeny and Laden were busy preparing for their crucial part in the plan. It was actually quite simple. He would be in the lab to help get people out at the opening above. Tweeny and Laden were going through the night stalker entrance with a few extra men for backup. If all went according to plan, they would not need a large contingent of men. Jom and Raini, would stay here to help guard the settlement in case things went very wrong.

He understood only too well the risks involved. They would be outnumbered, so it required stealth and timing to be successful. Satisfied all was ready, he got up from the table when he noticed Merlin hurrying toward him, excitement lighting up his face.

"We've got it," he said as he motioned Tanner toward the exit.

"She's sent the maps of the facilities?"

"Yes." Merlin said excitedly. "Will hooked up the communicator to his computer and he printed out all the maps. You need to come with me, so we can study them. They will be invaluable."

"Did she say when they would be ready to generate the field?"

"No. Just the maps."

"Let's go take a look at what's inside Cheyenne Mountain. We could be there within the week."

Sitting at the counter, back turned, Cara heard them leave. She was sure they hadn't really noticed her there. Tanner was deep in his thoughts when she arrived through a side entrance and Merlin had been so excited, he hadn't even looked her way. She had easily overheard them. Maps, within a week.

It was time to pay Dwight McGee a visit. She would claim a headache and take off this morning. As she stood to leave, she noticed two packed lunches sitting on the counter. Gertie and her helpers were back in the kitchen and no one was in the dining hall, so she grabbed the lunches and hurried out.

With maps strewn over a wide table, Merlin and Tanner sat intently studying them in Will's office. The dim light overhead gave them just enough light to see.

"Look here," Tanner exclaimed. "Here's the night stalker entrance. It's close to the lab, actually almost right under it. See where it winds around then branches off and up. Tweeny and the men can easily get to the lab along that corridor." Merlin looked where Tanner pointed and nodded.

"The Shell's residential area and offices are actually on the other side of the complex," Merlin said as he focused

229

back on the map in his hand. "Look at this large area in between. It's where the brotherhood resides." Tanner glanced at the map in Merlin's hand.

Grabbing another map, Tanner frowned. On the far side of the facility from the lab was the fertility clinic. It was actually above the Shell offices and residence. How were they going to get those women out of there? They didn't have the time to go all that way undetected, release them and bring them back. According to Elizabeth, many women were heavy with more than one child. If he had a way of transporting them, it might be possible.

By the time they finished looking through the maps, Tanner had a fairly good idea of the underground network of Cheyenne Mountain. Standing up to stretch, he patted Merlin on the back, telling him he would be back with Tweeny and Laden. Merlin nodded absently, still absorbed in studying the maps.

Cara came to the split in the trail. She turned left, heading west toward old Manitou Springs. Dwight had said he would be in one of the cabins north of the washed out town. As she drew near the cabins, she heard a branch break behind her. Twirling around, she spied him stepping out from behind a rocky outcrop, glancing suspiciously behind her. Satisfied she hadn't been followed, he lowered his gun and Cara ran excitedly to him, throwing herself into his arms.

"It's about time," McGee said irritably, hugging her quickly. "Any news and you got any food?"

230

Cara smiled as she pulled the lunch out of her pack. McGee grabbed it, heading toward the cabin. Once inside, he tore it open and swiftly began devouring the contents.

"What is happening over there?" he asked between mouthfuls, nodding in the direction of the settlement.

"They will be leaving within the week. They have maps of the inside of Cheyenne Mountain."

McGee swallowed hard. "Maps?" Cara nodded.

"You have to get them. I want the maps."

"That will be impossible. Don't you think they'll have them under lock and key?"

"I don't care. Find a way." McGee finished the lunch. "Got any more?" Cara grabbed the other bag out of her pack and handed it to him.

"You got any old shirts?" Cara asked.

"Why?" McGee asked as he pulled food out of the bag

"I need one to put in the woods outside the cabin so the wolves get a whiff of it. That way you can get close and they won't alert the guards."

"Good idea." McGee said as he finished off the second lunch. "Got anything else in there? All I've got is some canned vegetables on the shelves. Not much else in the way of food supplies."

Cara looked around the homey cabin. "This is nice. Was there someone here?"

"Nah. It was empty. Someone up and left right before I got here." McGee grinned.
There was something in his smug tone that bothered Cara, but she didn't say anything.

McGee stood up and found an old shirt lying across a chair. "Here. Take this." Cara stuffed it in her pack.

"I can't stay long. I don't want anyone to get suspicious. I'll be back with the exact day they are leaving. Do you know what a field is?"

McGee shook his head. "Why?"

"Tanner said something about generating a field." McGee looked at her strangely. He remembering hearing about a wave field that had caused this whole mess of a world they lived in. He couldn't understand why they would create the field again. He was going to find out, though.

Cara stood up to go. "Here are some jerky and extra rolls." She laid them on the table. Stepping close, she wound her arms around him. He crushed her to him and slammed his mouth against her, cutting her lip. She didn't care. After a few drawn out seconds, he pulled away.

"That will keep you till next time." He grinned down at her and turned toward the door. She followed and stepped out of the cabin. McGee stayed on the porch as she put her backpack on and headed toward the trail.

"Don't forget. We need the maps," he yelled after her. She turned to wave, but he had already disappeared into the cabin.

*   *   *

"Hey, where's my lunch?" Jom yelled out. "Anyone back there?"

"It's on the counter." A muffled voice replied.

"No, it's not."

232

A moment later, a head peeked out from the doorway to the kitchen. "Well, it was here." Elsa looked around. "I had them both sitting right here on the counter in their usual place, yours and Raini's. Hmmm. Hold on a minute. I'll fix them again." She smiled an apology.

"What's the hold up?" Raini asked from the dining room entrance.

"Just a little mix up. They thought they had made them."

"We did make them." The muffled voice again. Jom grinned at Raini who stepped up beside him.

A few minutes later Elsa was back with their lunch packs. "Someone must have taken them by accident," she said as she handed them to Jom and Raini. "That's never happened before. I'll start putting your names on them."

"Thanks," the twins replied together as they turned and left the dining hall heading to the cabin and outside.

"What was that all about?" asked Gertie, as she stepped out of the kitchen, wiping her hands on her apron. She walked over to the counter where Elsa was standing looking perplexed.

"Oh, I put Jom and Raini's lunch packs out earlier and they disappeared."

Gertie looked at Elsa thoughtfully. "You know, in the last few days, food has been disappearing. I thought I had miscounted, but now I'm not so sure. Keep your eyes open for anyone skulking around the kitchen." Elsa nodded.

Chapter Thirty Nine

Elizabeth stepped into the lab. After eating a quick lunch, she had hurried over, her excitement nearly bubbling over. Earlier that morning, they had concluded the last exhaustive calculations and integrated the remaining elements to complete the anti-gravity generator. They were now ready to test it.

She walked over to an upward slanting desk with a built in panel of buttons and switches in front of a wide section of the floor. Sitting down at the desk, she pushed a lever at the side of the panel. The floor in front of the desk ground open as the floor split, two sections pulling apart to reveal a large very unusual looking contraption: the TAG wave field generator. The splitting sections of floor ground to a halt and the unit began to rise.

The generator was approximately thirty feet in diameter. The whole assembly was encased in a circular low temperature vessel cooled with liquid nitrogen, so it wouldn't overheat. Sitting at the top of the vessel was a ring of super conducting ceramic made from yttrium-barium-copper oxide and layered with pure bismuth for stability along with one layer of magnesium zinc. The multi-layered ring would be set to spinning at 5,000 rpm.

Three electromagnetic coils were placed under the ring allowing the ring to levitate magnetically when it started its spin. Along with the precious element yttrium used in the ring, she had also obtained dysprosium and samarium, now being used in the enormous battery centered under the ring, the last component necessary to generate the field.

When the magnetic field became strong enough, it would be focused into space, directed toward the coordinates of the moon, creating a much different space. This space would be free of the force of gravity because the geometry that caused space-time gravity would be temporarily suspended. As a result of this, the moon would begin to accelerate toward the earth. She marveled at what this generator could do and knew it worked. It had worked before.

Once the moon reached the coordinates they wanted, the generator would be turned off and the moon would stabilize in its new orbit. An orbit close to the earth once again and that, in turn, would stabilize the earth's orbit.

Today, they would generate a weak field. She would put on the Icarus wings and fly just above the treetops. Once the field was generated she should fall automatically toward the opening. Vivien would turn it off before she fell into the generator. Once they successfully accomplished this test, they would be ready.

So absorbed in her work, she didn't hear Vivien and her father enter the lab.

235

"I see you're getting everything ready for the test," Vivien said excitedly from behind her.

"Yes. I'm nearly finished." She turned and grinned at her two favorite people. Well, two out of three. She could no longer deny her feelings for Tanner. She missed him. When she wasn't immersed in her work, which was most the time, her mind wandered to the time spent with him.

"I am going to get the wings." She stepped into the supply room. They didn't have much time. Norm, who could hack into any computer, was keeping his eye on Winston and Terrence's location. A message had just come in from Norm on her computer saying they were both in their offices right now and no one was heading toward the lab. It would take them at least fifteen minutes to get over here. The test would only take a few minutes.

Quickly putting on the wings, she hurried into the lab. The overhead passage was now open and Vivien gave her a thumb up. She began her ascent, flew through the opening and hovered about forty feet above it. The generator was turned on, but kept at a significantly weaker field.

Almost at once, Elizabeth fell from the sky. Vivien immediately turned off the field and Elizabeth stabilized right above the opening. She smiled down at her father and Vivien. It worked. They would be ready tomorrow night.

*   *   *

"Any word yet?" Tanner asked as he stepped into Will's office later that day. The communicator had been left there for safekeeping.

"Nothing." Will glanced up from studying the maps. "I was able to rig up another communicator for Tweeny. Once you're in the mountain, you will be able to communicate with him, using this one. Now that we have a secure band for communication, I think it wise you stay in touch with each other. I've already talked to Tweeny."

"Thanks Will. I'll be back later. Hopefully we'll hear from…" A beeping noise interrupted what he was going to say.

"We have an incoming message from them," Will said excitedly. "Hold on."

Will read the text message from the communicator out loud. "Tomorrow night at midnight."

Relief surged through Tanner. It was the waiting that was so difficult. "I'll tell the others." He turned to go, grinning at Will. "Thanks for all your help."

"Sure." Will grinned back.

Listening in the supply room outside the door to Will's office, Cara realized almost too late that Tanner was heading out of the office. She ran to the shelves in the back of the room and crouched down behind them. Tanner came out of the room just as she got out of sight. That was too close she thought. She still had to get to the maps sometime today. Time was running out now, as she needed to get back to Dwight by tomorrow with the news.

Glancing up, she saw Will leaving his office. He locked the door securely behind him as he went out. How was she going to get in there? She sat in the shadows, thinking about what she should do next when she heard faint voices coming from the corridor outside the supply room.

Within a heartbeat, she heard Tanner and Will entering the supply room. They stepped into the office, closing the door behind them. Deciding it was too dangerous to remain, and realizing there was no way she could get to the maps, she swiftly stepped out from behind the shelves and hurried out of the supply room. Maybe she could find something else of value to make up for the maps.

Inside the office, Will picked up the communicator, "Just as I was leaving, I got another message from Norm." Will handed the communicator to Tanner.

Tanner read it and grinned. "The new code to open the night stalker's door. I'll tell Tweeny and he can bring the controller over so you can program it in. That's great, one less thing to worry about. It looks like things are going just as we planned."

Tweeny found Tanner in Will's office the following morning. "Sorry to start the day with bad news," he said, "but someone broke into the armory and stole two guns,"

"What?" Who would do that?" Tanner looked at him incredulously.

Tweeny shrugged before continuing. "Gertie told me someone raided the pantry and stole bread and a pound of jerky. When I went to get supplies for our trip, I discovered we were short two flash lights."

Merlin walked in just then. "Marsha tells me Cara didn't show up for work today. She's not in her room and no one has seen her."

238

"Jom told me yesterday she was acting suspicious," said Tanner. "He saw her put a shirt in the woods further out on the trail and when he asked her what she was doing she said the wolves were growling at her. And now she's gone?"

"Maybe she decided she didn't want to live here after all and went back to the mutant camp," said Merlin. "Sorry, Tanner. I really thought she wanted to stay."

"Well, we can't worry about her right now," Tanner frowned. "It is better she's out of here before she did something worse than steal some of our supplies and weapons."

Dawn was streaking the sky when Cara reached the split in the trail and headed west toward the washed out town. She had easily sneaked past Merlin, asleep in the cot in the cabin. The guards in the trees had returned for the night, so no one saw her leave. Her pockets were heavy with the stolen guns and flashlights. Dwight would be so proud of her when she brought him the exciting news and extra supplies.

Last night her head had been spinning and she hadn't been able to sleep. As she lay in her bed, she realized she couldn't stay any longer. There was no reason to. Her place was at Dwight's side because he was her soul mate.

She knew she could talk him into letting her go with him because hadn't she proven how valuable she could be? Hadn't she been the one to get all the information? So what if she hadn't obtained the maps. She would make it up to him. Oh, she was going all right. Once inside Cheyenne Mountain, they would find the riches rumored to be there. What those riches were she wasn't exactly sure.

Chapter Forty

Elizabeth realized the day had slipped away as she nervously looked at the clock on the laboratory wall. It was late afternoon and she still wasn't done with getting all the loose ends tied up. The field generator was ready. That part seemed easy compared to the precise timing it would require for everything else to fall into place.

Needing a break, she stepped out of the laboratory and into the hallway. She headed toward the cafeteria for some much needed coffee. The hallway was bustling, everyone preparing for the upcoming battle. Instead of looks of excitement, most people had either a blank or fearful, apprehensive look. Elizabeth remembered when things had been different, when a spirit of camaraderie and starting anew was in the air. Not anymore, not since the Spencer brothers had turned Cheyenne Mountain into Residuum and become dictators, although no one used that word.

After getting her coffee and situating herself back in the lab, she noticed a message from Terrence. It was blunt and to the point: We marry tomorrow in the Brotherhood Hall at 10:00 pm. Elizabeth immediately erased it. In your dreams, she thought to herself. I don't plan on being here.

If they could pull it off, project moonshine was happening tonight at midnight, not tomorrow night at 9:00 like Winston and Terrence thought. They had purposely left that change of plans out. If they were able to successfully return the moon to its orbit and escape, they would be one step ahead of the tyrants. She knew many of the people here were forced to cooperate, either through threats to their family or the chips in their brains. Winston and Terrence did have some support and they would not go down without a fight. The more people out of the influence of those two, the more guarantee of success in defeating them.

Going over the plans once again in her head, she knew a number of things could go wrong. What if Winston or Terrence came to the lab? She shook her head. Elizabeth knew they rarely left their rooms after 11:00. They could send

241

a guard to check the lab. If they were found out, it would be over for them. They would be forced to finish the project tomorrow night and they would probably be eliminated immediately after its completion. She was sure Terrence would personally kill her with his bare hands. She shuttered at the thought.

"Elizabeth, are you okay?" So deep in her fears, she hadn't heard Vivien enter the lab.

Elizabeth sighed. "I was just thinking about everything that could go wrong."

Vivien walked over to Elizabeth and put her arm around her shoulders. "We have to believe everything will go right. Remember, we also have Tanner and his men helping us."

"I know. We are taking such a risk in going against Winston and Terrence. I'm afraid for us, for everyone."

"It's all set in motion," Vivien replied. "It's too late to turn back."

"I know. I wouldn't want to do that." Elizabeth took a deep breath and smiled. "Besides, how else are you and Merlin going to reunite unless we escape this prison?"

"Exactly. Now let's finish up in here and get some rest. We've got a few hours before Tanner shows up. We're going to need all of our attention and focus to get this right."

Tanner looked around him at the men gathered in the library by the back entrance. Even though the day had passed at a tortuous pace, the sun inevitably set and they were prepared to leave. He would fly to the opening and join the others in the lab while his men went through the back entrance and into the night stalkers den. There were twenty men, including Tweeny and Laden They were sorely outnumbered, and if anything went wrong, he might not see them again. Stealth was on their side and if their timing was perfect, they would succeed.

"Keep your communicator on, Tweeny. I will be in the lab by the time you get inside. I will keep you posted." Tweeny nodded.

Tanner stood at the back entrance and shook every man's hand as each one headed out. Tweeny and Laden stopped in front of him. He grasped each of their hands in turn and they nodded, no words needed. It was time. Following them out the entrance, Tanner watched them disappear into the stygian darkness of the forest, their footfalls growing more distant until silence enveloped him.

He looked above him at the brightest star in the dark sky but that was no star and the reality of the evening hit him like a punch to his gut. If all went as planned, the moon would be back in its orbit this very night, traveling its ancient path around the earth, once again illuminating the deep darkness of the night sky. He took one last lingering look and stepped back through the door. He needed to get ready.

"Merlin, it's too dangerous."

"I can back you up. You have so few men. Elizabeth said they have hundreds at their disposal. I can help."

"I need you here." Tanner walked over and put his hand on Merlin's shoulder. "I will bring Grandma back. I promise." Searching Tanner's eyes, Merlin slowly nodded.

Reaching into his pocket, Merlin pulled out a small box. "Will you give this to Vivien? It was supposed to be her good luck charm twenty years ago, but I never had the chance to give it to her."

He opened it for Tanner to see. Inside was a necklace. Hanging on a gold chain, a diamond-encrusted circlet sparkled and at its center hung a luminous crescent moon cut from a rare pearl. With the pearl's soft inner glow adding to the elegance of the necklace, it was exquisite. Tanner whistled softly.

Merlin closed the box and handed it to Tanner. "Tell her this gift has been a long time coming."

Tanner nodded and tucked it safely in his shirt pocket. "It's time to go. Let's head to the back entrance. Help me with the wings." Just then, Jom and Raini showed up to say their goodbyes. They all trudged out the back.

Once Tanner had the wings situated, Merlin handed him his rifle. Along with that weapon, Tanner also carried a gun it its holster around his chest and a knife strapped to his leg. He had rounds of ammunition in a belt around his waist. After hugging each of them, Raini stepped back and wiped a tear from her eye and sniffled once, but she quickly gained her composure.

Merlin wished him luck and they all shouted encouragement as Tanner rose. Then he was gone, disappearing quickly into the dark sky. Turning around, they slowly stepped back inside, fear gripping them like a vise.

244

Not so much for themselves, but for the people they loved dearly.

Chapter Forty One

Elizabeth returned to the lab, too nervous to sleep. It was now nearing ten and Tanner would soon be here. The hallways had quieted down and the few people she saw didn't look twice. People were used to her going to the lab at all hours and assumed she was preparing the field generator for tomorrow night. If only they knew.

Vivien and her dad were already there when she arrived. They looked as stressed as she felt. Sitting in front of the panel, she glanced at the instruments.

"We did a final check right before you got here," said Vivien. "Everything is a go."

"Norm has taken over the grid," added her dad, grinning. "Anyone looking at it will see a lab with no one in it."

"Good," replied Elizabeth. "It's just a matter of timing now." She nervously looked at the clock again, the third time in two minutes.

They all heard the noise from above and looked up at the same time. Tanner swirled down through the open portal and landed with a thud hard on his feet. "I need to work on my landing."

That seemed to ease the tension in the room and they all quietly laughed as Vivien hurried over for a hug. He quickly took the wings off and put them on a nearby shelf ready for use when they began hauling people out of there.

"Is everything on schedule?" He stepped back to the panel where everyone was gathered.

"Yes," answered Vivien. "When the moon is back in its orbit, the people who want to escape will show up here and we will begin the evacuation. By morning, everyone will be gone."

"Oh, Grandma, I have something for you." Tanner reached into his pocket. "A gift from Merlin." He handed the small box to Vivien.

246

"It's lovely," murmured Vivien, as she opened the box and gazed at the necklace inside. Eyes glistening with tears, she clasped it behind her neck. The hanging moon glittered in the light.

"Merlin has been holding on to that for twenty years. Something about a good luck charm."

Vivien laughed. "We definitely need a little of that."

"What if someone walks in during the field generation?" asked Tanner.

"Norm will warn us," replied the professor. "If it's a guard, we'll tell him we're checking the system. We are in here at all hours so it won't seem that unusual. Of course, you'll have to hide. He might wonder where you came from."

Just then Tanner's communicator let out a quiet beep. He stepped into the storage room and returned a few minutes later. "That was Tweeny. He's at the back entrance and waiting my signal."

"The timing needs to be precise for everything to go according to plan," Elizabeth murmured, as she checked the system again. "A quiet beeping came from the panel. "It's time to start the field generator." She pulled a lever up and the ring began spinning.

"Once it reaches 5,000 rpm, I will activate the battery and the anti-gravity field will be on. Within five minutes, an electromagnetic anomaly of space will be created thus sending the moon towards the earth. It will take approximately thirty minutes to reach the correct orbital coordinates."

Elizabeth checked the speed of the ring and nodded. "Here we go."

"Hey, what are you doing here?" the guard yawned. "I never see you here this late."

"I couldn't sleep," replied Terrence, as he stepped over to the monitor. "Too much excitement in the air. Everything running smoothly?"

"Yeah, it's quiet around here. Not many people out and about."

Terrence glanced at the grid. Everything looked normal, no one in the lab. The guards were all at their stations. He might as well go back to his room and get some sleep. He took one last look and headed for the door.

"Oh, congratulations. I heard you're getting married tomorrow," the guard yelled after him.

Somewhat annoyed by the guard's comment, Terrence turned at the doorway. The guard sat grinning at him and behind him the lab monitor flickered. The flicker caught his eye and for just an instant Terrence saw figures in the lab huddled over the panel, then the image was gone. The lab was empty again.

"What was that?" He walked over to the monitor.

"Huh?" The guard turned and studied the grid. "Everything looks normal to me," he said with relief.

"No. No, it's not." He pushed the guard out of the way and tapped repeatedly on the grid keyboard. Nothing. The lab looked empty. "I know what I saw. There is someone in the lab." The guard looked at him in confusion.

248

Fear overtook Terrence. "No, they wouldn't, not tonight. This can't be. It was all planned for tomorrow night when our satellite would not be in the affected space. Oh, God, not our satellite. No, it's impossible." The guard stared at Terrence.

Don't they know the satellite will be destroyed? He froze. Of course they do.

Elizabeth sat monitoring the screen. "It's working," she said excitedly. "The moon is approaching and their satellite is burning up in earth's atmosphere. There goes their GPS and mind controlling chips."

"I'm contacting Tweeny now." Tanner said. He went into the storage room, closing the door so as not to distract Elizabeth.

Tweeny answered at the first ring. After talking briefly to Tanner, he turned to Laden. "The satellite's destroyed. Let's go." Laden nodded and took the lead.

Once inside the corridor, they swiftly ran toward the night stalker's sleeping area, their flashlights bouncing off the sides of the walls.

When they got there, Laden yelled out. "You are free. The Gods are dead. They can no longer hurt you. The Gods are dead. We have destroyed them. You are free."

There was a confusion of rising bodies, looking around, startled. Many were tilting their heads as if listening for a message. Then they sat or stood frozen, not attacking, just waiting.

Laden approached one he knew by name. "Sands, remember me. It's Laden. We have come to help you escape. The Gods are no longer able to speak to you in your head. We need to destroy them completely. We must get into the mountain."

Sands came out of his stupor. "We must obey the Gods. You cannot pass this way."

"Listen, we are here to help you. Can you hear them in your head?"

Sands paused, listening. "No, but they will hurt us if we help you. They always come back."

"Not this time," Laden replied. "We have destroyed them completely. Believe me. I have lived without them in my head since I escaped. You can too."

The others were beginning to rise. They began chanting. "Kill the intruders." The men raised their flashlights and the night stalkers backed away.

"Listen everyone. We need your help to stop the Gods completely. Many of you know me. I escaped and my friends here helped release me from the Gods. They took them out of my head. Now we have done the same for ..."

An alarm began wailing loudly.

Elizabeth looked at the others in confusion. A text from Norm came on the screen. *There was a glitch in the masking program. They saw you in the lab.* Before anyone could react, Terrence was inside the room next to the panel. He yanked Elizabeth off the chair and held her in front of him with a gun pointing at her head.

"Everyone step back." The professor and Vivien carefully backed up. "You all think you're so smart, don't you?" Terrence asked derisively. "Thought you could outwit me. Not this time."

"It's too late," the professor said cautiously approaching Terrence. "Your satellite is destroyed. You will have no control over the people anymore. Put the weapon down."

"Shut up, old man. It's never too late." Terrence hit him on the side of the head with his gun and the professor went down in a heap, then he jammed the gun into Elizabeth's head. Tanner stood behind the door which he had managed to crack enough to see, but he couldn't get in a good shot without jeopardizing Elizabeth's life.

"If it's over for me, it's over for you, too," Terrence continued with a sneer. "What will happen if you don't shut down the field generator, huh?" Elizabeth looked at Vivien in horror.

"Exactly. If I'm going to lose everything I've worked for, so will you." A bell chimed from the panel sounding a warning. Three minutes to lunar orbital coordinates.

"That's insane," Elizabeth pleaded. "We can start over. It's not the end, just the beginning."

"For you maybe," Terrence said with contempt. "The world is mine to control. You were mine. Now, it doesn't matter. I will win in the end." The warning bell sounded again. Two minutes to lunar orbital coordinates.

"What will happen to your precious earth when the moon collides with it? It will be over for everybody. You thought you could win against me? You are all so incredibly stupid." His eyes burned with anger as he tightened his hold on Elizabeth.

Fear iced Tanner's spine. From his vantage point, he could see the terror in Elizabeth's eyes, but she was positioned right in front of Terrence. He pointed his gun at the arm around Elizabeth's neck. There was no way he could make that shot safely. If he didn't do something they would all be dead anyway. The warning bell again. One minute to lunar orbital coordinates.

As he stood there, desperately trying to take some kind of aim, knowing the only shot would hurt or kill Elizabeth, a shot rang out. Elizabeth slid to the floor, blood splattering the side of her head. Terrence lost his balance and fell backward. Ten, nine, eight...the computer was counting down the seconds to the lunar coordinates. Tanner froze, unable to comprehend that Elizabeth was shot.

Five, four, three...Tanner sprang into action and raced toward the panel, the bell clanging loudly. The moon had descended to its new orbit. The generator had to be turned off immediately. Vivien seemed paralyzed, staring at Elizabeth's fallen body.

Not knowing what to do, and at this point frantic about Elizabeth, Tanner yelled at Vivien to help. As he approached the control panel, a dazed Elizabeth slowly sat up, pulled herself to the panel and pushed a lever. The alarm stopped and the generator turned off. The ring began slowing down. Elizabeth slid back to the floor.

Shaken but alive Elizabeth looked up at Tanner and smiled weakly. Blood splattered the side of her neck and shoulder. It wasn't her blood. Tanner stared at her, marveling at the fact she was intact and unharmed. Terrence lay behind her, a bullet through his head, his blood pooling on the lab floor. Elizabeth gestured toward the entrance of the lab. There stood Winston, the gun in his hand now pointing at them.

"Unfortunately, things did not work out precisely as planned," Winston stated dully, gazing at his dead brother. Sounds were coming from the corridor. Tanner hoped it was Tweeny and Laden.

As if shaken out of his remorse, Winston turned to the others. "My brothers and I are leaving." Nine young men rushed in behind him, abruptly stopping when they spied their brother's dead body. Eight of them were in the wings. The one in front held out a pair for Winston. They were all laden with heavy packs and supplies.

"Please drop your weapon," Winston said to Tanner. Tanner did, not wanting to risk anyone's life. "You will let us leave because I am taking Elizabeth for assurance."

"No." Tanner yelled, the knot is his stomach twisting even tighter.

"Yes," Winston calmly answered. "Unknown to my brother, we have a plan B. I couldn't let him destroy the earth. Not now, when we have the moon back." He glanced at Terrence's dead body sprawled on the floor. "Sorry, brother." A flicker of emotion appeared in his eyes; it was quickly gone as he turned his blank stare back to Tanner.

"We will leave her on the trail outside the entrance," Winston said as he pulled on the wings.

"How do I know that?" Tanner responded, frightened for Elizabeth.

253

"You have my word." Winston replied, as if that was enough.

"Your word? What is that worth?" Tanner asked incredulously.

"I just killed my brother." His voice was laced with pain, although his face revealed nothing. "You would be dead now, all of you, if it wasn't for me. I am offering you an alternative to that. You will just have to trust me. Anyway, why would I need an astronomer now?"

Despite Tanner's misgivings, something in Winston's voice convinced him. He nodded, desperately hoping he didn't regret it.

Winston smiled smugly. "I knew we could come to an agreement." His wings secured, he prepared to leave.

"I'm not going," a voice called out at the back of his brothers.

Winston shook his head without turning. "Ace, you were always a rebel. I won't force you and I'm certainly not killing another brother."

He turned to study Ace. "Suit yourself. You can be of some help, though. Please use your gun to guard this group for a few hours, at least. Enough to get a reasonable head start."

He looked back at Tanner. "I have lost this battle, but it's not over. And I do detest killing an unarmed man."

He grabbed Elizabeth, her eyes wide with terror. "She should be easy to spot. After all, you have the light of the moon now." With that, he rose slowly and swept out of the opening with his brothers following one by one.

Vivien knelt down to check on the professor. He was starting to come to, groggily opening his eyes and moaning. Someone cleared his throat at the opening.

"I'm terribly sorry to be pointing this gun at you," Ace grinned good-naturedly. "It's really not like me. However, they do need somewhat of a head start I suppose."

Chapter Forty Two

An hour later, still under Ace's watchful eye, Tanner's stress was steadily increasing. His concern over his men was growing and he was extremely worried about Elizabeth. His men should have been here by now and Elizabeth's whereabouts was unknown. Would Winston keep his promise? Earlier, guards had rushed in, but Ace had assured them everything was in order and had sent them off to other areas of the complex. The alarm had ceased, probably Norm's doing.

The professor was sitting in a chair and after Vivien inspected his head, she walked into the supply room and brought back a blanket. She gestured toward Terrence's body. Ace nodded and walked over to grab the blanket and place it over his brother.

Tanner was slowly edging toward the entrance, listening for his men. He turned back toward the lab as Ace covered the body, suddenly looked up and stared woodenly in Tanner's direction. He carefully raised his gun, pointing it directly at Tanner.

Shocked at Ace's response, Tanner cringed, eyeing the weapon. "Hey, I'm not going anywhere."

Ace pulled the trigger.

The blast echoed through the lab.

Tanner clasped his chest, instantly realizing there was no gaping hole. Was Ace that bad of an aim? Hearing a thud behind him, he spun around to see Dwight McGee lying crumbled in a heap, blood spreading across the front of his jacket, a loaded gun still clutched in his hand.

Ace calmly walked over. "A friend of yours?"

"No. Not really."

"It bothers me to no end when someone is aiming a gun at an unarmed man's back."

256

Tanner felt a surge of gratitude. "Thank you. You saved my life."

Ace shrugged. "Now, I need to deliver a message on the intercom. I believe it is still in order. Powered locally and all."

"What kind of message?" Tanner asked warily.

"I'm not like my brothers. The people here need their freedom. I know that. I have seen what my brothers created and I don't like it. That is why I stayed, to help you."

"To help us? You don't know us."

"I know Elizabeth and you are her friends. That's enough."

Vivien pointed to the wall where a phone was attached. "Push the intercom button and the whole complex will be alerted."

Ace nodded and stepped over to the phone. His voice reverberated throughout the underground complex. "Citizens of Cheyenne Mountain hear me. This is Acely Shell." Tanner raised an eyebrow; Ace shrugged.

"Put down your weapons. The intruders are not here to kill or enslave you. They are here to free you. Terrence is dead and Winston has fled. The microchips inside your heads have been de-activated. You are free from them. They will soon be removed. Citizens, put down your weapons. There is no battle here. It is over. We are free."

"Does that freedom apply to me?" Tanner asked.

Ace sighed. "I think my brothers have enough of a head start. Besides, I don't think it's them you'll be looking for."

"You're right. I need to find Elizabeth. I hope your brother keeps his promise."

Ace shrugged. "It was always one of his best traits." That did not lessen the unease in the pit of Tanner's stomach.

A smattering of bullets could be heard in the distance then it was quiet. Approaching footsteps sounded down the corridor. Tweeny rushed into the room, nearly tripping over McGee's body. It was then he noticed Ace with his gun pointed directly at him. "Whoa! I'm on your side, I think."

Tanner nodded at Ace and he lowered his weapon. Laden rushed up behind Tweeny, taking in the scene. "We saw Cara hysterically running toward the night stalker exit," Laden said. "We couldn't understand what she was doing here."

"She and McGee must have followed you here. McGee was going to shoot me in the back." He gestured toward Ace. "This is Ace. He's the reason that worthless lump of flesh is blocking the entrance. How is it they managed to get here before you?'

"All hell broke loose when the alarm went off," Tweeny explained. "Laden couldn't reason with the night stalkers so we ran and we must have missed the turn. They had us cornered and we kept them back with our flashlights. When they heard the message, they backed off."

Looking around, Tweeny's gaze took in Vivien and the professor. "Did it work? Where's Elizabeth?"

"I was just leaving to find her," Tanner replied. "And yes it worked. Vivien will fill you in on the details." Tanner stepped into the supply room to retrieve the wings."

258

Stepping back into the lab, he strapped on the wings. Ace grinned. "I should have known you had an extra set of wings."

Tanner nodded. "Will you guys bag the bodies? Is there somewhere we can store them until we bury them?"

"Yes. We have a storage unit for the deceased."

"Good." He gave his phone to Vivien. "I think there is someone you need to talk to." With that, he was gone, out the top of the mountain.

Looking up he saw it, high in the eastern sky. Tanner's breath caught at the sight above him. Elizabeth had truly achieved the seemingly impossible. The moon once again cast its light over the earth. It was almost full and shone with a brilliance Tanner had thought he would never see again. He wanted to take it all in but he couldn't; he was too distracted with worry over Elizabeth and he needed to focus his attention on the landscape not the sky.

Winston was right. The light from the moon illuminated the landscape, making the trail easier to see. Guilt and remorse filled Tanner. He shouldn't have let her go, shouldn't have trusted Winston. There was no one below him. He saw what looked like someone huddled beside the trail, but on closer inspection it turned out to be a gnarled log. Where was she?

What if Winston blamed her for having to kill his brother and changed his mind. Maybe he took her with him or worse. Tanner frantically searched the trail. I can't lose her, he thought. Not now, when everything we worked for has turned to success. Not now. He prayed to a god he didn't think existed until recently.

His eyes and ears were playing tricks on him. He saw movement when there was nothing. There, over there, someone was waving. It was just a branch, moving in the wind. He heard someone crying. It was the wind. Panic hit deep in his chest and surged upward. If Winston hurt her, he would search for him and kill him with his bare hands.

Without warning, a green glow briefly lit up a wooded area off the trail; just as quickly, it was gone. If he hadn't been looking directly at the clearing, he would have missed it. He landed on the trail as close to the light as possible. Quickly pulling the wings off, he lumbered through the woods, tripping over logs and rocks. His flashlight was of no use. The batteries were dead.

"Elizabeth, are you here," Tanner yelled. The only sound was the wind whispering in the trees. He stumbled into a clearing and a body lay curled in the grass.

Tanner rushed over. Elizabeth was bound and gagged lying on her side, her eyes closed. He couldn't tell if she was dead or alive.

Tanner quickly removed the gag and the ropes that bound her. He checked for a pulse and found one. Relieved, he gently gathered her in his arms. Her eyes flickered once, twice and then she was staring wide-eyed at him, confusion written on her face.

"Where am I?"

"You're safe. It's over."

Relieved, Elizabeth tried to rise up; her head pounded. "I think someone hit me with a rock after dumping me here." Sudden fear swept over her features. "Is my dad all right?"

"He's okay. Everyone is safe. You accomplished your mission." Tanner felt gently along her head for any sign of injury. "You have a good-sized lump at the back of your head but there's no blood."

"At least, I didn't lose my memory this time." Elizabeth relaxed back into his arms. "How did you find me?"

"I saw a green glow. It was only for an instant, so I almost missed it. I don't know what it was."

Elizabeth laughed weakly and raised her arm. "My watch. I put neon in it. Every hour it glows brightly to remind me of the time."

"Only a scientist would do something like that," Tanner chuckled. He then grew somber. "I thought I had lost you. I…Winston…I couldn't…"

"Stop. It wasn't your fault. I'm fine, just a little disoriented." Elizabeth looked around her. "Can you help me up?"

Tanner gently lifted her and set her on her feet. Knees weak, she wobbled and swayed. He pulled Elizabeth into his chest, wrapping his arms around her. The intensity of his gaze took Elizabeth's breath away. Moon shadows danced in the wind.

"I thought he lied," Tanner whispered hoarsely.

"No. He dropped me off like he said, just not on the trail. I don't think he wanted to make it too easy to find me. You know, I think it's a game with him, and he still wants to play it."

"What did he say?"

"Nothing really," she frowned with a sudden thought. "Oh, just before I got clobbered he did say thank you."

"Thank you?"

Elizabeth pointed upward into the night sky. "For that, I think." They both raised their faces to the moon, drinking in the sight. The rich lunar light cast a golden glow into the clearing where they quietly stood. Arms wrapped around one another, they bathed in the true joy of a moonlit night.

Chapter Forty Three

When Elizabeth and Tanner finally returned to the complex, a chaotic scene greeted them. Ace was barking out orders. People were coming and going in the lab. Tweeny was tilted back in a chair, grinning as he watched the scene unfold.

"It's about time you got back," he grinned even wider. "We thought we'd have to send out a search party. We had plenty of volunteers. It seems everyone wants to go outside now."

"I can understand that. It's a beautiful sight out there," Elizabeth said, gazing at Tanner. He smiled back. The powerful moment they shared outside under the moon filled them both with a deep sense of elation and wonder. A moment neither of them would ever forget.

"Ace here is trying to restore some order," Tweeny said. "He sent Laden off to the night stalkers to calm them down."

Ace's speech had worked. It didn't take much to convince the guards to lay down their weapons. They had been living in fear of Winston and Terrence for too long, being threatened into submission or given chip implants to guarantee their obedience.

Fortunately, many people knew and liked Ace. Unknown to his brothers, he had been sympathetic to the people living in Cheyenne Mountain. He just didn't know how to help them until now. Many had cheered after his announcement.

"Merlin will be here tomorrow," Vivien said, her voice breaking. "He is going to start taking out the chips and checking on the pregnant women. I can't believe it is finally over. No more living in fear. We are finally free."

Vivien wiped her eyes. "He was sitting outside on the steps when I called. He watched it all, saw the moon go from a bright point in the sky to…" Vivien's voice broke. "Sorry, I'm overcome with joy."

Elizabeth ran over to hug her father as Vivien continued, "Merlin said the young people were in awe. Of course, they had heard the stories and seen pictures of the moon, but they couldn't believe their eyes when they actually saw it. It seems everyone was cheering and crying. No one wanted to go back inside."

264

"Grandma, it's because of you." Tanner said. "The three of you, you never gave up. You were willing to go to any lengths to succeed, and you did. We now have a chance at a real life here on earth."

Vivien clasped her necklace. "What about Winston?" She whispered, her voice tense. "He's still out there. He may have lost this battle, but he'll be back."

"When and if he returns, we'll be ready," Tanner answered. "Now, I think we deserve a celebration, in honor of the success of Operation Moonshine." Everyone laughed, nodding in agreement.

Ace looked around in confusion. Laughing, Tanner slapped him on the back. "When you have some time, we will tell you all about it."

73984595R00164

Made in the USA
Columbia, SC
08 September 2019